"God, you're beautiful."

Sam's voice was unsteady as he tightened his arms around her, drawing her close to his hard body.

"No, Sam," Meg protested, twisting away. But when he turned her face to meet his kiss, her response was strong and immediate. All resistance, all anger melted with the sweetness of his mouth on hers.

It had always been like this. Her reaction to him was as fiery and breathless as the first time. Pressing against him, she felt his arousal, and her body was aflame with longing.

Suddenly, with a soft laugh, Meg pushed him down onto the bed. "Let me..." she whispered.

Dear Reader,

We at Harlequin are extremely proud to introduce our new series, **HARLEQUIN TEMPTATION**. Romance publishing today is exciting, expanding and innovative. We have responded to the ever-changing demands of you, the reader, by creating this new, more sensuous series. Between the covers of each **HARLEQUIN TEMPTATION** you will find an irresistible story to stimulate your imagination and warm your heart.

Styles in romance change, and these highly sensuous stories may not be to every reader's taste. But Harlequin continues its commitment to satisfy all your romance-reading needs with books of the highest quality. Our sincerest wish is that **HARLEQUIN TEMPTATION** will bring you many hours of pleasurable reading.

THE EDITORS

U.S.
HARLEQUIN TEMPTATION
2504 WEST SOUTHERN AVE.
TEMPE, ARIZONA
85282

CANADA
HARLEQUIN TEMPTATION
P.O. BOX 2800
POSTAL STATION "A"
WILLOWDALE, ONTARIO
M2N 5T5

Love Me Again

ELISABETH MACDONALD

Harlequin Books

TORONTO • NEW YORK • LONDON
AMSTERDAM • PARIS • SYDNEY • HAMBURG
STOCKHOLM • ATHENS • TOKYO • MILAN

To my cherished friend,
Aileen Ehlers

Published July 1984

ISBN 0-373-25118-1

Printed in Canada

1

MEG DRISCOLL rose from the stone bench in front of the small brick air-terminal building, and resumed her restless pacing. She'd been waiting twenty minutes for the director of the Forest Grove Shakespearean Festival to pick her up. The college town's airport was small, with only two scheduled flights per day. Surely the festival people knew her time of arrival. Impatiently, she glanced at her watch, then looked in vain for a taxi.

Nearby, two workmen mending a fence stopped to gaze appreciatively at her. Meg was used to men looking her over like that. She'd long ago accepted her beauty as part of her stock in trade as an actress and model. Unlike her acting skills, it was not something she could take credit for, so it remained of minor importance to her.

Slightly taller than average, Meg's slender figure was clad in a natural-linen pantsuit and a raspberry-colored silk blouse. She made a striking picture. Her dark brown shoulder-length hair flashed with golden highlights in the June sunshine as she turned to check her watch against the clock above the terminal doors. A frown creased her forehead between long-lashed hazel eyes, to be replaced by a sigh of relief as she saw a station wagon heading toward the air terminal.

The automobile screeched to a halt in front of her, and a rotund little man bounced out from behind the wheel. "You're Margaret Driscoll," he cried, bearing down upon her with his hands outstretched.

"Dr. David Worth, I presume," Meg said, her irritation vanishing as Dr. Worth kissed her hand. He reminded her of her mother's schnauzer, Max. Tufts of thinning gray hair stood upright where he had swept a nervous hand over his head. Gray-white sideburns curved around his plump cheeks to end in a tiny beard. His dark eyes snapped with restless energy. This was the man who'd built the Forest Grove Shakespearean Festival from nothing into a prestigious, world-renowned event.

Meg's agent, Jerry Greene, had said, "They're small, but solvent. Your paycheck won't bounce like it would with a lot of summer-stock companies." But Meg wasn't easy to convince. She had done summer stock before, and she was still hoping the TV pilot she'd done several months ago would be picked up. Jerry, however, had refused to listen to her arguments for staying in Los Angeles.

"The prestige of another summer of repertory Shakespeare will look good on your resumé, honey," he'd insisted. "Besides, right now I have nothing for you. And you'll be only a phone call and a two-hour plane ride away if something comes up that won't interfere with your performances."

Jerry was right, of course, Meg realized bitterly. Her career hadn't exactly zoomed since she'd arrived in Los Angeles a year ago to take a minor part in a TV

soap opera. It had been written out after six weeks,
even though she'd been assured of a long-term role.
There had been a happy six weeks when she'd done a
small part in *Plaza Suite* at the Mark Taper Forum
Theater. Afterward, she'd done a few bit parts in TV
movies before the role in the still-untitled pilot came
along. She'd managed to survive by modeling when-
ever Jerry could find a commercial for her. At least
she'd worked fairly steadily at acting, which was an
improvement over the situation she'd left in New
York. It was only a matter of time and luck, she kept
telling herself, until the right break came along and
success would be hers.

"Sorry I'm late," Dr. Worth was saying. "The
plane usually isn't on time...and I'm sure you can
appreciate what a hassle it is getting the rest of the
company settled." Quickly he turned to grab her two
suitcases, then stowed them in the back of the battered station wagon bearing the logo of Forest Grove
College. "There now!" he said, and opening the door
for Meg, bowed her into the car.

With a jerk that made Meg question her chauf-
feur's driving ability, the station wagon pulled away
from the curb. In a moment they had joined a small
stream of traffic moving toward town.

"You'll make a marvelous Desdemona." Dr.
Worth's bright eyes were taking inventory of her, ignoring the traffic around him.

Watching Dr. Worth's appraisal of her, Meg
smiled knowingly. "I'm looking forward to it." At
least the good doctor's attention seemed to be purely
professional, and that put her at ease. "I worked with

Harold Devore at Shakespeare-in-the-Park in New York," she went on. "He's a very talented director, and it'll be wonderful to work with him again."

A sudden change in Dr. Worth's effusive manner, the rather tentative smile he flashed her, made Meg edgy. Something was not quite as it should be. "Has Harold arrived?" she asked.

"I have some rather unsettling news," he began, looking even more like a nervous schnauzer. "Harold's had a heart attack. He's still in the hospital in New York City."

"Oh, no!" Meg said. "Will he be all right?" Her edginess turned into deep concern, not only for Harold, but herself. The fact that he would direct had been the deciding factor in her decision to take this job.

"The prognosis is good, I understand. But he'll be out of commission for quite some time." Again the tentative sidelong glance. "Fortunately we've been able to obtain the services of an equally well-known director. He's a good friend of Harold's and since he was free this summer, he agreed to take over for Mr. Devore."

Trying to conceal her disappointment, Meg sighed, knowing she'd signed a contract and she was stuck with whoever had taken Harold's place. It might prove a pleasant summer anyway, she thought, looking out the car window at the tree-shaded college town they were passing. The Rocky Mountains to the east shone in the setting sun, and it struck Meg that she had forgotten the sky could be that lovely shade of cobalt blue.

"Who'll be directing *Othello*?" she asked curiously, turning her attention back to Dr. Worth.

He cleared his throat. "Sam Richardson."

"Sam!" She shouldn't have cried out his name like that. How could she have guessed the very sound of it would tear open wounds she had thought were healed? Surely Dr. Worth knew she had once been married to Sam Richardson. No wonder he was so hesitant about divulging his news. Panic seized her. She'd call Jerry right away! He had to get her out of this contract. The change in directors should be reason enough.

For one brief aching moment she was lost in remembrance of those enchanted days and nights she'd shared with Sam. Tumbling through her mind like a kaleidoscope she saw Sam's blue eyes grow dark with passion as they looked down into hers. She could almost feel the magic his hands wrought on her body as the fierce flame they kindled together consumed her. No! She wanted to cry out the word as pain mounted inside her. Meg was sure she could never survive a summer of working with Sam. Dr. Worth should have known—but how could he? How could anyone know how she'd loved Sam, how their parting had torn out a part of her heart?

"I realize you and Sam are divorced," Dr. Worth was saying in a placating voice. "But I'm sure you're both professional enough to not let that interfere with your work."

He'd struck the right note, Meg thought grimly, staring straight ahead as the car turned through the entrance of the green rolling campus. Its old brick

buildings were softened by ivy, the paths crowded
with students hurrying between classes. If there was
anything she prided herself on, it was her profes-
sionalism. She'd never been late for a filming or an
audition or even a rehearsal, and she always knew
her lines. Just the same, she'd call Jerry. She couldn't
bear to be near Sam for a whole summer, working
with him, remembering what they'd had and what
they'd lost. When she first left him, she'd let the bitterness consume her. Then, simply to survive, she'd
forced the memories from her mind. Until this moment, she'd managed to pretend she no longer cared.

What an actress you are, she told herself, unable to
stem the flood of anguish. *You even made Meg Driscoll believe she wasn't still in love with Sam Richardson.*

Blind to the lush beauty of the college campus,
Meg found herself remembering that first audition
after she'd come to New York from Northwestern
University drama school, determined to succeed as
an actress.

SAM HAD been directing an off-Broadway play that
was being cast. Even in memory, she felt an electric
thrill pulse through her when his piercing blue eyes
met hers as she stepped onstage. Waiting for her turn
in the auditions, she'd watched him—a tall rangy
man who moved with the grace and ease of an actor,
his voice authoritative, his manner direct. He had a
nervous habit of running his fingers through his thick
sandy hair until it looked disheveled. Searching for a
word to describe him, Meg chose "charismatic." He

had that indefinable something that drew men and
women alike, gave him authority and charmed
everyone into doing his bidding. She liked the rugged
planes of his face, the sprinkling of freckles on his
nose and his bare arms. When she read the part, she
knew she was reading for him alone, and that she had
never done better.

Sam was smiling as he helped her step down from
the stage. "We'll call you," he said, looking deep into
her eyes.

He called that night. "The part's yours," he announced, sounding pleased. "Will you have dinner
with me tonight?"

Meg's heart leaped. She had a room in a run-down
boardinghouse with a pay telephone in the hallway.
Most of the roomers were actors, and every time the
phone rang, doors opened and hopeful faces appeared, each one waiting for the magical summons to
the theater.

Cupping her hand over the mouthpiece, hoping no
one could hear, Meg asked, "Are you one of those
'casting-couch' directors I've heard about?" She was
only half joking, hoping in her heart that he was not.

Sam's laugh boomed over the line. "That kind of
thing makes life too complicated," he chuckled. "Although I must admit you tempt me, Miss Driscoll.
How about it? I can't afford the Four Seasons, but I
know a good spaghetti joint where wine comes with
the dinner."

Later, seated opposite Sam, Meg looked around at
the red-checked tablecloths, the candles stuck in
empty wine bottles, the wooden floors sprinkled with

sawdust. "This place looks like a set for an Italian café," she said with a smile.

Sam nodded. "Maybe that's why I like it. A lot of theater people hang out at Mama's. Not those who've made it, of course, just the poor ones on their way up."

"We hope!" Meg exclaimed.

"Yes, we hope," Sam repeated, lifting his wineglass to her. His deep blue eyes were warm with admiration as he watched her across the table. After he had ordered spaghetti for both of them, he asked, "How long have you been in New York?"

"Does it show?" She gave him a wry grimace. "I've been here three months and thought I'd acquired a veneer of sophistication."

Sam laughed. "Afraid not, Meg. You still have a glow of innocence. Most actresses tend to lose that after they've been around for a while." He paused, looking at her with serious eyes. "I hope you never do."

The genuine caring in his rugged face touched her so, it was a moment before she could reply. She said lightly, "Well, thanks to you, I have my first professional acting job. Now I can begin to practice looking shopworn."

"Don't!" There was a harsh edge to his voice. "You're perfect just the way you are."

Their eyes held. Meg felt the pulse at the base of her throat begin to pound.

Sam broke the moment, reaching to refill her wineglass. "Margaret Driscoll, real name," he recited. "Studied drama at Northwestern, twenty-two years old, born in Rockford, Illinois... worked as a model in Chicago and New York.... What else?"

"A typist," she said with a laugh. "My practical father insisted I learn to type when he knew I was determined to become an actress. I'm registered with a temporary office service and it's paid the rent a few times."

"Smart father," Sam commented. "Did your mother go along with that?"

"Not really." Meg smiled, thinking of her loving, if flighty, mother. "She always wanted to be an actress, too. She's a fixture in amateur theater back home. It was all she ever did before she got married." She gave Sam a wry look. "Of course she's certain her daughter will be a big star and never need to know how to type."

"She may be right." Sam gave her an intense look that seemed to set her blood afire.

Taking a deep shaky breath, Meg sipped her wine. She'd had plenty of male admirers back in Chicago. None of them had ever affected her like this. Every fiber of her being was aware of this man. Always before, she'd been too intent on preparing for her career to become emotionally involved. At this moment, it almost seemed as though Sam had been here waiting for her.

A handsome Italian waiter brought their spaghetti. Meg learned from his conversation with Sam that, like most of the people who worked at Mama's, he was an aspiring actor. When he departed there was a brief silence while they devoted themselves to the pasta with clam sauce.

"You have an advantage over me," Meg said finally. "I didn't get a chance to read *your* resumé. I've heard you're making a name for yourself as a director. Where are you from?"

"I grew up in New York City," he replied. "I was lucky enough to win a scholarship to Yale drama school. Finished there about six years ago. Never wanted to do anything but theater. I tried acting, but I have this weakness—I like to be in charge. That's why I'm a director."

"You don't have much of a New York accent," she said.

"The advantages of stage training." He grinned. "My dad was a postman, now retired and living in Connecticut with my mother and my little sister who teaches school there. At first dad didn't approve of my choice of profession. He was overprotective, I suppose." He paused to sip his wine, then added with a smile, "Now, every opening night he's there applauding his hands off. They all do, even my career-army brother when he's in town."

"Sounds like a great family," Meg observed with the envy an only child often feels toward big families. "Didn't your dad make you learn to type?" she added mischievously.

Sam gave her his lopsided grin. "No, but I've paid the rent working on a construction crew more times than I care to remember."

"Construction." Meg was delighted. "That's what my dad used to do in the summers. He said it cleared his head after a winter of trying to teach English to high-school students." With a wry laugh, she continued, "Even though he taught me to love the classical theater he wasn't too thrilled when I decided to become an actress. I think he really wanted his darling daughter to get married, settle down and raise grandchildren."

"Wait till he sees you in this play," Sam told her earnestly. "It's the kind of part that could get you noticed where it counts, even if it is off Broadway." He leaned back and looked at her, appraising. "You have a quality that's pretty rare, believe it or not. It's called class, and has no definition."

"You're very kind," she murmured, pleased. She wanted his approval, wanted him to like everything about her.

"Nope," he disagreed amiably. "You'll find when we get to work that I'm definitely not 'kind.' I can be a real bastard, but I love the theater and I think anyone who's in it owes it their very best."

Stirred by an idealism and dedication that matched her own, Meg gazed into his incredibly blue eyes. "I think so, too," she said softly. For the first time she knew someone other than her father who truly shared her love for the theater.

He reached across the table to take her hand in his. Feeling the radiant warmth of that clasp, she glanced at his hands. They were big, strong, with long sensitive fingers, sandy hairs curling on the back and a sprinkling of freckles as endearing as a child's.

They might have been alone in the dim café. Meg was aware only of his touch, his eyes holding hers, the air between them charged with emotion. A fragment from Shakespeare floated through her head:

"No sooner met but they looked; no sooner looked but they loved."

"As You Like It!" she said aloud without thinking, then laughed joyfully at Sam's puzzled expression.

Together, they walked back to her boarding-house, discussing the play, sharing hopes and dreams for the future. When they stood on the steps with the tangy odor of autumn in New York all around them, Meg thought she couldn't bear it if he didn't kiss her.

Gently, Sam drew her to him, cupping her chin in one hand. His lips brushed her forehead, moved down her cheek, touched the sensitive spot beneath her earlobe.

"I always make it a rule," he murmured, "to not get involved with the actresses I'm directing."

"Yes?" Meg sighed, her whole body yearning to draw closer to him, aching to feel his lean strength against her.

"Every rule has to be broken sometime." His mouth took hers in a kiss that left her senses reeling. Her bones seemed to dissolve. Meg leaned against him, answering his kiss with a passion that aston-ished her. Sighing, Sam released her. Still dizzy, Meg reluctantly left his arms.

"Rehearsal at ten," Sam said, and in two long strides he was down the steps and whistling off down the dark street.

As his tall figure blended into the darkness, Meg stood in the half-open doorway, watching. She had an irrational impulse to call after him. He'd told her his apartment was just around the corner. They could be alone there, she thought suddenly, in each other's arms.

You're out of your mind, she scolded herself. *You've only just met the man!* Then, the line from *As You Like It* went through her head again: "No sooner looked but they loved."

Long before the five weeks of rehearsal were over, Meg knew she had found her mate, as certain they belonged together as she had been that first night. Sam was one of a kind. She loved the way he lived and breathed theater, claiming nothing could replace the experience of shared emotion flowing between actors and a live audience.

During the weeks of rehearsal Sam and Meg often shared dinner at Mama's. On bright autumn days there were picnics in the park. And there were embraces that Meg found increasingly difficult to terminate.

When Meg met Sam's parents on opening night, she was quickly drawn to his sweet-faced mother and his gentle father. If Sam's dad regretted his son's choice of profession, it wasn't evident. He overflowed with pride. They sat in a booth with Sam and Meg at Mama's after the performance, waiting for the reviews. When the papers arrived, Mr. Richardson called the *Times* critic a "damn fool" for his less-than-kind review, and Meg fell in love with him, too.

A rosy dawn stained the eastern sky by the time they had seen Sam's parents off on the train to Connecticut. In the chill autumn morning, Sam and Meg walked back toward her boardinghouse. Sam's arm was around her, holding her close against him.

Disconsolately, Sam said, "If that damn Fitz had rewritten the third act like I wanted him to.... Maybe if I'd cast a more experienced actor in the lead.... If...."

"Don't Sam." Meg looked up into his weary face. She had been concerned about the reviews too, even though her part had not even been mentioned. It was Sam's play, and its success was important to him. A tremor went through her as she realized how deeply she loved this man. The play was not what mattered to her. What mattered was Sam's happiness and success. The desire to comfort him, to love him, shook her so that she felt herself trembling against him.

"You can call a rehearsal this afternoon and start repairing the play," she told him, letting her lips graze the edge of his chin when he turned to look down at her. "Right now, you need some sleep."

Sam looked startled, only then aware that she had steered him to his apartment building rather than her boardinghouse around the corner.

"Meg?" he asked tentatively.

"Darling," she replied.

Holding on to each other, they walked the three flights up to Sam's tiny untidy apartment. Once inside, he put the chain on the door and took her in his arms. After the long night of rising hope and crushing disappointment, Meg gave herself to his kiss as she never had before. With mounting passion intensified by long denial, they explored each other, disrobing as they moved toward the bed. Every sense aflame, Meg responded to Sam's embrace. It seemed to her she had loved him forever, longing for this moment when all her love could be expressed in the ultimate intimacy.

Tenderly, Sam caressed her, leading her slowly from one plateau of desire to the next. Wild with longing to possess and be possessed, Meg was barely conscious of the brief sweet pain as they came together. Their bodies moved in sensuous rhythm until that incredible moment when Meg's whole being was shaken by an ecstasy that threatened to tear her apart.

"Sweet Meg," Sam murmured as they lay sated and breathless in each other's arms.

"My love," she answered, and thought she would drown in his deep blue gaze as he repeated the words like a vow.

"My love."

MEG MOVED in the next day, knowing she was doing exactly what her father had always feared. Nothing seemed to matter except being with Sam, loving him through the early hours after they came from the theater, waking to love him again in the afternoon light.

The play closed a week later. At Mama's, after they had shared a last meal with the other members of the cast, the two of them lingered on, drinking red wine and talking.

At last Sam said, "Well, we're both out of a job, the rent's due next week.... It's a hell of a way to begin, but I want to get married, Meg."

"Oh, Sam," she gasped, wanting him with all her being, but never having quite hoped he would consider marriage at this point.

Taking her hand, Sam kissed each fingertip carefully. The slow sweet arousal his caresses always brought flowed through her as she watched him lovingly.

"I love you, Meg." He was very quiet and serious. "And I happen to be a guy who loves once and forever. I know you've had a lot of pangs of conscience about moving in with me. It seems we're a couple of conventional people in an unconventional business. I want to be able to say, 'this is my wife,' not 'this is my lady,' or whatever the current euphemism may be."

"Darling," she whispered, aching with love. "Are you sure?"

His lopsided grin made her heart turn over. "I'm sure," he said softly. "Will you, my love?"

"Yes," she murmured, leaning across the table to meet his kiss. "My love. . . ."

THE SQUEAL OF BRAKES as Dr. Worth drove into a parking lot brought Meg back to the present. She didn't want to remember all that—had sworn she wouldn't. Now Sam was here. She had to get to a phone and call Jerry at once.

"We'd like to be able to put our stars up in a fancy hotel," Dr. Worth said, as he unloaded her suitcases. "But we do have to stay within budget. I'm sure you'll find the student housing quite adequate."

He led Meg from the parking lot through a breezeway to the flagstone patio filling the space in the center of a U-shaped one-story building. Sided with rough-sawn cedar, it was reminiscent of a motel.

With an apologetic laugh, Dr. Worth continued, "This complex is reserved for married students during the winter. Eventually the college will replace it with a multistory dormitory, when they have the money." He paused to unlock the door of one of the apartments, insisting, "It's really very nice."

Meg looked around at the huge oak tree shading the patio where lounge chairs and tables were grouped. A high trellis draped with red rambling roses separated the patio from the street beyond. The whole scene had an inviting restful air. *It doesn't matter*, Meg told herself. *I won't be here.* Her eyes fell on the telephone booth in the breezeway.

The apartment was very small, with a combination kitchen-dining area, a living room with a sofa, chair and desk, and a tiny bedroom with a bed, night table and chest of drawers built into the closet wall.

"Since we're not pressed for space this year, I thought you'd prefer to be alone," Dr. Worth said, turning on lights and opening windows like a bell-boy. "The cafeteria is nearby, or you can stock the kitchen, as you wish."

"Thanks. It's very nice," she said, anxious to get to the telephone, thinking she wouldn't even bother to unpack.

JERRY WAS DECIDEDLY uncooperative. "I don't even have a lead on anything here," he said emphatically. "If word gets out that you've broken this contract, that you're uncooperative, then you've put me in a hell of a bind. Come on, honey," he coaxed, "you can put up with Sam for the summer. I've heard he's a nice guy."

"Sure," she snapped, "you weren't married to him." She slammed down the phone.

"Oh, damn!" Meg said as she shut the door behind her and dropped into the armchair. She looked around the drab little apartment with its beige walls, beige rug and beige plaid draperies. For some reason all that beige reminded her of the last furnished apartment she'd shared with Sam, and unbidden tears filled her eyes.

Like a film being rerun before her eyes, she saw herself a year ago in that New York apartment, packing her things, furious at what she could only think of as Sam's betrayal, while Sam sat on the worn sofa bed and got quietly drunk.

There was a knock at the door. With a start, Meg realized she was sitting in a strange apartment in a Rocky Mountain college town noted for its Shakespearean festival, all alone, tears streaming down her face.

The door opened before she could speak. A pixie face topped by a mop of red-gold curls peered through the crack.

"Hi! I'm Carol Gould, your next-door neighbor." She opened the door a little wider. Seeing the tears on Meg's face, she clucked sympathetically. "This place really isn't that bad. You ought to see how I've fixed mine up. Just think of it as summer camp."

Laughing, Meg found a tissue and wiped her eyes. "Feeling sorry for myself doesn't accomplish much," she said. "Come on in."

"No, thanks." Carol gave her a gamine grin. "Just wanted to remind you the festival committee is throwing a bash for the company this evening. Buffet dinner and wine in the theater courtyard at six. Want to go with me?"

"Sure," Meg agreed, responding to Carol's warmth, trying to ignore the sinking feeling that reminded her she'd have to face Sam at this party. "Let me shower and change."

MEG CHOSE a cream-colored silk dress with a wide swirling skirt and a ruffle-trimmed bertha collar, the rich pale color complementing her dark coloring.

"Wow!" Carol said, as they walked across campus to the replica of the Globe Theatre where the festival took place. "You'll make a gorgeous Desdemona. That is, if you can stand that egotistical ass, Zach Stone, who's playing Othello."

Meg groaned. "I met Zach when I lived in New York, and I know what you mean."

"I get to play Bianca, the whore." Carol laughed, imitating a sexy walk. Her slender figure in the girlish green-and-white-print dress made the effort so incongruous that Meg laughed aloud.

"The part of Mariana in *Measure for Measure* will make up for it," Carol continued. "Especially since Payton James is directing. He teaches at the University of Washington where I'm taking my master's degree in theater arts, and I'll confess right off—I'm madly in love with him."

Meg smiled at her companion, liking Carol more every minute. Ahead of them, lights gleamed in the grove of pine and fir trees where the theater complex was located. The pleasant murmur of voices beckoned through the cool spring dusk.

"If I wasn't," Carol was saying, "I'd be after Sam Richardson. God, he's wonderful. And he isn't even handsome."

Silent, Meg felt a strange sense of loss, remembering when she had thought Sam the most wonderful being on earth. *You're an actress,* she admonished herself, *a damn good one, and you're going to have to act twenty-four hours a day for the next three months.*

Carol rattled on about the company and the plays, adding tidbits of gossip about the actors and actresses. She had been here two days and already knew everyone.

"Here we are," Carol announced as they walked through the wrought-iron gates into the theater courtyard. "Come on, I'm dying of thirst." Carol moved toward the table where a bar had been set up.

Meg stood quite still, looking over the milling crowd of actors, actresses, directors, designers, dancers.... She saw the top of Sam's head, bent to speak to someone, the unruly sandy hair looking like he'd been in a windstorm. Then his intense blue gaze met hers across the dimly lit courtyard. Meg's heart lurched painfully and seemed to cry out the words forever engraved there: my love.

2

"Ah! My Desdemona!"

Meg tore her mesmerized gaze from Sam and turned to face Zachary Stone. She'd known him slightly in New York and found him too egotistical to be interesting. Zach was tall, with dark wavy hair and chiseled features so perfect they seemed unreal. He wore a navy blazer, light gray trousers and tattersall vest, the epitome of Brooks Brothers splendor.

"Hello, Zach," she said pleasantly, aware that they would have to establish some kind of rapport if they were to work together. He'd grown a beard since she'd last seen him, presumably for his role as Othello. It gave him a sinister look that suggested the villain Iago rather than the noble Othello.

Zach's dark eyes moved in obvious appreciation over her figure and he grinned suggestively, showing perfect capped white teeth in his suntanned face. Holding his wineglass aside, he bent to whisper in her ear, "Anytime you want to make the beast with two backs, baby!"

It took all Meg's restraint to not slap his smirking face. Clever as he thought he was, propositioning her in Elizabethan terms, he needn't think she was about to fall into bed with him. She'd learned from experience that sometimes the easiest way to deal with an unwelcome pass was to ignore it.

"Would you mind getting a glass of wine for me?" she asked, thinking she would wander off while he was gone. But Zach merely turned and hailed a passing waiter, handing Meg the glass as though he'd done her a great favor.

"Thanks," she said coolly, sipping the chilled white wine, wishing he would move on. But Zach stayed beside her, occasionally waving and calling to acquaintances in the crowd.

The courtyard was centered by an enormous old maple tree and paved with antique brick. A riot of colorful petunias glowed from huge clay pots set around the area. Dim houselights gleamed from the open-air theater beyond, and hurricane lamps flickered on the buffet table opposite. Around the courtyard, gas torches added to the pleasant ambience.

"Surprised to find who's directing *Othello*?" Zach asked, arching his dark brows in a meaningful way.

Meg shrugged. Refusing to rise to his obvious baiting, she answered, "Of course, but I do hope Harold's going to be all right."

Zach smiled at her over his wineglass. "I would have bet you'd turn around and take the next plane out when you found Sam was here—after what happened in New York."

In desperation, Meg looked around for someone to rescue her from the conversation. Carol was deeply engrossed in a good-looking man with gray hair. Dr. Worth was busy setting up a microphone on the stage. Finally, she said, "Oh . . . and what is supposed to have happened in New York?" Her cold sarcasm didn't seem to ruffle Zach.

"Well," he continued in a gossipy manner Meg found offensive. "It's common knowledge that Sam broke up with you just when he had his first big success with *First Generation*."

Meg's fingers tightened on the wineglass. Her lips ached with the tight smile she kept on her face, presenting a cool facade to Zach's curious eyes. Zach knew nothing of what had really happened in New York. He was merely repeating gossip and digging for more.

She had left Sam before *First Generation* opened off Broadway, long before the play's success moved it to a big theater uptown. Of course, she was glad Sam had a hit, Meg had told herself when she heard the news. She thought, with a twinge, that if it had come sooner, perhaps she and Sam would still be together. But if success and money were necessary to hold a marriage together, it wasn't much of a marriage.

Ironically enough, their story could be the plot for a play about the struggle for success on Broadway. A talented young director meets a beautiful young actress—they fall in love—and their relationship is destroyed when one finds success at the expense of the other.

IN THE THREE YEARS they were married, their careers had followed the usual ups and downs. Meg had landed parts in two off-Broadway shows. One ran a month, the other closed immediately after opening. They had both enrolled in Harold Devore's class in Shakespearean interpretation, which led to a summer at Shakespeare-in-the-Park, and from there, the next summer, to a stint at the Stratford Shakespearean Festival in Connecticut. The third summer, Sam was Harold's assistant director at Shakespeare-in-the-Park. He'd been involved in several off-Broadway plays, none of them successful.

Occasionally, Meg had found it necessary to take a typing job to pay the bills. But there were more and more calls for her to do modeling. She had never liked modeling—it seemed so mindless. But it paid the bills. Many a time she had to pass up an audition because she had a modeling assignment. Sam was always totally involved with the theater. When he wasn't working, he would get a group of actors together, all anxious to practice their craft, as Sam was practicing his.

Gradually, after that first ecstatic year, Meg began to resent Sam's devotion to the theater. She'd thought she was devoted too, but Sam put his work before everything else. Meg never confided her uneasiness to Sam. She knew that until he came up with a really successful play, he couldn't support them. Complaining wasn't Meg's forte, the money from modeling was excellent, and if she loved Sam she had to believe in his ultimate success as much as he did.

Her agent had been able to get a toothpaste commercial for her. It was so successful her face seemed to pop up on TV every time she turned it on.

"Not exactly great theater," Sam said when he

walked into the living room and saw the commercial for the first time on their second-hand television set.

"It pays the bills," Meg retorted, wishing she hadn't turned the television on.

"Hey, love." Sam's voice was placating. "I didn't mean—"

"I know what you meant," Meg interrupted. "You're a damn snob about theater."

Furious, she pointed at the fade-out of her smiling face next to the blond child who played her daughter in the commercial. "If you think it didn't require acting skill to work with that little brat. . ." she ground out, breathless with anger, remembering the agonizing hours working with the spoiled girl and her demanding mother.

Quickly, Meg switched off the television. She hated the damned ad. Why couldn't Sam understand that she resented the whole thing because it wasn't what she wanted to be doing. Tears of indignation stood in her eyes.

Picking up a pillow from the sofa bed, she flung it at Sam, who caught it. With a grin, he flung it back at her, then followed it to take her in his arms. For a moment, she was so angry she didn't even want him to touch her, but slowly the warmth of his kisses, the familiar caressing hands replaced the heat of anger with a growing flame of passion. Before she quite realized how it happened, Sam had flipped open the sofa bed and they were naked in the middle of it, making love and laughing together.

End of act 1, Meg thought ironically, sipping her wine, suddenly aware that Zach was still talking.

Zach's mouth was moving but she wasn't hearing him. The noise of the party seemed far away.

WHEN FIRST GENERATION came along, Sam was certain this was his long-awaited big break. It was the best thing he'd ever done, he kept telling Meg. The playwright worked with him as though they were one mind. But the show was short of cash and Sam was working without a salary, struggling to bring the play to opening before the backer's money ran out.

Even though it meant passing up an important audition, Meg accepted when her agent called with an assignment. She was to model for a catalog put out by a mail-order women's fashion store. Although she didn't mention the lost audition to Sam, it rankled in her heart. Sam's enthusiasm for the play began to irritate her, too, even though she wanted him to succeed. She longed to be in the theater with him, doing the work she loved. But modeling did pay some of their bills.

They were always short of money, she thought bitterly as she climbed the stairs to their tiny walk-up apartment after a long and tiring day in front of the cameras. Opening the door, she heard Sam in the kitchen. He came out holding an open bottle of wine. Two steaks rested on the chopping block beside the stove.

"Welcome home, love!" Sam cried happily. "I just saved the play. We're celebrating."

"That's great," she said, responding to his kiss, wanting to share his joy in spite of her weariness. "Did you find an angel somewhere?"

"Didn't you always think my dad was an angel?" He laughed, taking two wineglasses from the cupboard and pouring the wine.

"Your father?" She stared at him, aghast.

"Sure," Sam replied jauntily. "He's invested in my play."

"Oh God, Sam!" She ignored the glass of wine he offered and turned away to fling her coat over a chair. "How could you? Your father's retired. He's on a pension. He can't afford to invest in off-Broadway plays...even for you."

"He made a little money in the stock market," Sam said, his exuberance dying at her reaction. "You know he's my greatest fan. He read the play and loved it. And he insisted, Meg. He *demanded* that I let him do this—for me, and he said, for him. He's always wanted to be involved in the theater."

"You shouldn't have taken his money," she retorted. "I can't believe this." She saw anger flood Sam's face. "I can't believe even you would be so selfish."

"Do you think I asked him for it?" Sam's voice rose. "Or that it was easy to take his money? He wanted to do it. He claims he's not taking any bigger risk than he would in the market."

"Oh hell, Sam," she said furiously. "Why didn't you take that offer to direct a TV show? How long are we supposed to go on starving for *your* art, living on borrowed money?"

"Dad believes in me." Sam's voice was dangerously quiet. "Even if you don't." For a moment he stared angrily into her cold face, then turned away, gulping down his wine.

"I have to be at the studio by six," Meg said. She heard the bitterness in her voice and didn't care. Turning her back to Sam, she began changing her clothes. "I need to get to bed early. Cook the steaks your dad paid for...although it's beyond me why you couldn't have settled for hamburger."

The steak and the wine were like dust in her mouth as they ate in silence. Sam often did the cooking when she was late, and he was a good cook. But tonight there was no joy in their meal, no sharing of the day's activities, no discussing plans for tomorrow.

After dinner, Meg showered, washed and dried her hair while Sam cleaned up the kitchen. The quarrel hung heavy between them in that little apartment. For the first time in three years, they lay rigid beside each other in the sofa bed, wide-awake, an impenetrable wall of resentment and misunderstanding separating them.

Staring into the darkness, Meg thought how she had come to love Sam's family. It was obvious Bob Richardson adored his youngest son. Meg often wondered if Sam wasn't living out his father's deepest dreams...dreams long ago discarded in the necessity of supporting a family. Surely Sam knew that. How could he have used his own father's money, knowing that most off-Broadway plays never turn a profit.

Because he's selfish, she thought in frustration, turning her back to him. Anything for the theater, his first and most obsessive love. She was tired of being the breadwinner, always playing second fiddle to Sam's career. The good reviews she'd received for her Juliet at Shakespeare-in-the-Park had brought her a lead in an unsuccessful off-Broadway play. She was failing to establish herself as an actress, and at twenty-five her modeling career couldn't last much longer.

Frustration overwhelmed her, anger at Sam simmering beneath it. She sighed, trying to clear her mind, courting sleep so the fine lines at the corners of her eyes wouldn't require extra makeup in the morning.

When the modeling session ended the next day, the store's advertising manager asked Meg and three other models to stay. The company had decided to fly them to Nassau to do outdoor shots for the catalog. Could they all leave the next day for Nassau? It would probably be a three-day shoot.

Meg agreed, thinking she needed to be away from Sam. This would give her some space to think over what was happening to their marriage. Right now, her disillusionment with him put a pall on everything. Surely she couldn't have so completely misjudged him.

That evening when he came home to find her packing, her heart leaped at the sight of him as it always did. She saw that he was annoyed at her news. His kiss was perfunctory.

"We're opening Friday," he said. "You knew that."

"I'll be back," she replied. "Good old Meg. You can always count on me."

There was a long silence while Sam stared at her as though he wasn't sure what to say next. Meg continued packing, not looking at him. Finally Sam went into the kitchen and put a frozen dinner in the oven.

"I have to go back to the theater," he called to her, "to go over some things with the lighting director." He came to the door, giving her a tentative smile. "Wait up for me?"

"Our plane leaves Kennedy at five forty-five," she said coolly, knowing he wanted to come home and make love to her; wishing she was as eager as she had once been; and hating the resentment that had cooled her ardor.

When Sam let himself into the dark apartment, undressed and got into bed, she was still awake. She turned to him, wanting desperately to erase this thing between them, wishing it had never happened . . . that it was a year ago when they were crazily in love, still holding reality at bay. There was something of that desperation in their lovemaking, as though they both longed to recapture the past and drown their fear of the future.

"My love," Sam whispered afterward. "My dearest love."

Entwined in the beloved body she had come to know as well as her own, her head cradled on his broad shoulder, Meg clung to him. In the afterglow of passion, she could almost believe nothing had changed between them.

ALMOST A YEAR HAS GONE BY NOW, Meg reminded herself, as the old pain welled inside her. Her life with Sam had ended. Why had she let Zach's snide remarks bring it all back, flashing through her mind in an instant? Only vaguely aware that Zach was still talking, she thought miserably, that was act 2, and then there was the final scene.

THE CATALOG photographer knew Nassau well and had his shots blocked out in his mind before the plane landed. As a result, the shoot went quickly. There was no time for the models to bask in the sun or swim in the warm ocean.

Meg moved mechanically through her posing, her mind preoccupied with Sam. By the time the photographer called it a wrap a day early, she had determined to go back and force Sam to frankly face their situation. She would make some demands of her own and try to save their marriage.

Walking up the stairs to their apartment, Meg was full of hope. She hadn't been open with Sam about her resentment. If they could sit down and talk it over honestly, surely they could find their way back to what they once had. Maybe he could even make her understand why he had been willing to risk his father's savings in his play. Smiling, she turned the key in the lock and pushed the door open.

Sam had obviously had guests, but that was not unusual. Their apartment was a gathering place for young theater people. Ashtrays were overflowing and empty glasses stood on tables. Now there were only two people in the apartment. The overhead lamp in the little dining alcove shone as brilliantly as a spotlight on the two figures.

Sam was mixing a drink at the table where bottles and empty glasses stood in disarray. The girl was Linda Parker, the lead in *First Generation*. She stood behind Sam, her face pressed against his back, her arms around him, hands moving suggestively over his body.

Meg dropped her suitcase. Linda gave a little gasp

and stepped away from Sam, who turned around. With both hands outstretched he came toward her. "Meg, love...welcome home!"

Sickness built inside her until she feared she might faint. Meg stared at him, unable to speak. She had come home with such hope—to find this!

Sam's voice seemed to come from far away. "I had some of the cast over after dress rehearsal. Linda and I were just having one last drink before I took her home."

The room wavered before Meg's eyes, pain blurring her vision. Somewhere inside a despairing voice cried, *Not this! Not this too!* She vaguely felt Sam's strong hands on her shoulders. The telephone rang and she jerked away from him to pick up the receiver.

"Josh Greene here," said her agent. "Glad you're back, Meg. I just had a call from my brother, Jerry, out on the West Coast. He's got a TV producer who fell for your toothpaste commercial. He wants you for a small part in his soap opera, 'Today We Live.' It could work into a bigger part. Soap operas are using high-powered stars nowadays."

"In Los Angeles?" Meg asked, not recognizing her own voice. In the background, she was dimly aware of Sam and Linda talking...Sam helping Linda on with her coat...Linda setting her highball down on the coffee table, then the door closing behind her.

"Right," Josh was saying. "This could be a big break, honey. What do you say?"

Meg raised her head from the telephone to see Sam still standing by the door, watching her warily.

"When do I leave?" she asked Josh in a tight voice. As she listened to his arrangements, her eyes fell on Linda's lipstick-smeared highball glass, half-empty. Anger and hurt boiled up inside her until she thought she would scream with the pain of it.

With a shaking hand, she picked up the glass. Josh's voice faded in the distance as she raised her arm and threw with all her might. Sam ducked and the glass shattered against the door, the pale amber liquid dribbling slowly down the scarred beige paint.

3

ZACH WAS STILL TALKING, Meg realized with a start. It was a moment before she could subdue the pain of her memories and reorient herself. She was standing in the shadow of an Elizabethan theater in a Rocky Mountain college town . . . and Sam was there, across the courtyard.

"He must've made a bundle," Zach was saying, with what Meg detected was a hint of envy. "He had a piece of the show so the money must keep coming in even though he left it to direct *The Stamp Collector*."

"Also a hit," Meg said, enjoying the fact that Sam's success seemed to irritate Zach.

"I hope you got a decent settlement out of him." Zach waited for her answer, his dark eyes gleaming with malice.

Meg merely gave him a stage smile, wondering whether she should be rude and tell him it was none of his business. She'd refused to take any money at all, even after *First Generation* was a hit. She didn't want to be beholden to Sam in any way. Then too, she felt that Sam should pay back his father's loan first. It would have been unbearable if he had lost his father's life savings. The disappointment she had felt then came harshly back to her. Success didn't minimize Sam's lack of honor in taking the money...or in his relationship with Linda.

Unwilling to stoop to Zach's level, she finally said in a cold voice: "I'm happy for Sam's success. And as for working together, we're both professionals."

"Of course." Zach smiled and took a bottle of wine from a nearby table to refill Meg's glass. With a shock, she realized that in her annoyance she had gulped down her wine.

Zach turned to gaze around the courtyard. "I suppose the good Dr. Worth will get around to introducing the company before dinner is served. That's Joan Gaffney with Sam. Have you met her?"

"No. I arrived only two hours ago." Meg's eyes rested on the voluptuous blonde standing very close to Sam, looking up into his eyes. He'd always told her he preferred her sleek slenderness to full-bodied women, but it seemed obvious now that his eyes were devouring Joan's décolletage. The pale green peasant-style dress she wore was certainly inviting.

Sam himself looked elegant in a well-tailored brown suit with a white shirt and burgundy tie. A sick pain swept over Meg and she recognized the ugly symptoms of jealousy.

Zach chuckled. "I've never figured out what it is about Sam that women like. They seem to flock to him. Joan, for instance. She's been coming on to him ever since she arrived." He sighed and grinned playfully at Meg. "And to think she could have had me for the asking."

"You're impossible, Zachary," Meg said, and

laughed when she saw he had taken her words as a compliment. She knew now how to get along with him. Zach was far too self-absorbed to recognize a putdown, but it would be easy enough to keep her distance.

The shriek of a microphone being adjusted echoed through the courtyard. Dr. Worth had taken his place on the platform and was waving his arms for attention.

"Ladies and gentlemen! Welcome to the twentieth anniversary year of the Forest Grove Shakespearean Festival," he proclaimed with a broad smile. "Although I doubt it, there may be some of you who aren't aware of the history of this festival." He paused, and with a twinkle added, "Anyway, I'm determined to tell you the whole story."

Twenty years earlier, he explained, a group of amateurs had produced two of Shakespeare's plays on this same outdoor stage, to immediate acclaim. Since then, the size of the festival had grown steadily, until through a generous endowment, they had been able to construct a replica of the Globe Theatre, where performances now took place. The building was now world-renowned for its authentic appearance.

"Of course it all takes money," he said in a meaningful voice, and introduced the president of the board of directors.

Alexander Martin was an attractive man of medium height, with thick salt-and-pepper gray hair. His impeccably tailored light gray three-piece suit was in sharp contrast to Dr. Worth's rumpled navy blue one.

"Welcome to the new Globe," he said, his deep warm voice hardly needing the aid of the microphone. "Otherwise known as the Louise Moody Martin Theater. My mother, who was one of the founders of the Forest Grove Shakespearean Festival, would have been thrilled to see where it has gone from such humble beginnings. We're delighted to have you all with us. Dr. Worth never fails to choose a worthy company. May this season be even more successful than last."

Dr. Worth took the microphone again, after shaking Alexander Martin's hand enthusiastically. Turning to the audience, he said, "The success of this festival owes a great deal to Alex and his mother, whose generosity funded the building of our theater. We couldn't do it without you, Alex." Lifting his hands over his head, Dr. Worth encouraged the applause. Alex Martin merely inclined his head in a modest manner before he stepped down from the stage.

Expansively, Dr. Worth looked over the crowd. "I feel the company we've assembled this year is the best we've ever had. Since it would take all night to introduce everyone, I'll limit myself to the directors, because you'll all need to know them. I will be directing *The Comedy of Errors*." With a smile, he bowed to the polite applause. "My good friend, Dr. Payton James, will be directing *Measure for Measure*."

The gray-haired man standing beside Carol waved at the crowd and grinned ingratiatingly.

"I might add," said Dr. Worth, "that Dr. James has brought a number of his students from the University of Washington drama school to join our company."

Meg caught Carol's eye and nodded in approval.

"Last, but far from least," Dr. Worth went on, "we are honored to have the successful Broadway director, Sam Richardson, with us to direct *Othello*."

Sam acknowledged the applause with a wave. Watching him, Meg felt her heart turn over at the familiar lopsided grin.

"Each year," Dr. Worth continued, "we try to stretch our budget to include at least a couple of Equity members. This year we're privileged to have with us the beauteous Miss Margaret Driscoll, and that urbane gentleman, Zachary Stone."

Zach bowed to the polite applause, the picture of cool sophistication. Meg put on her most brilliant smile and waved at the crowd. She wouldn't look at Sam, she promised herself, but in spite of her resolve, her eyes were drawn to him. His deep blue gaze held hers as he lifted his wineglass in salute. The wistful smile he gave her was so unlike Sam, it stabbed at her heart. For a moment their eyes remained locked, then Joan took Sam's arm and turned him away to meet someone.

Accepting a glass of wine from one of the hostesses, Dr. Worth returned to the microphone. "The ladies of the festival guild are signaling frantically that dinner is ready, but first I'd like to propose a toast." He raised his glass, and the audience in the courtyard returned his salute. "To the world's finest Shakespearean festival, and to a successful season for our twentieth anniversary." As though reluctant to give up center stage, Dr. Worth finished, "Eat, drink and be merry, for tomorrow we start cracking the whip."

Amid the burst of laughter, the crowd swirled around. Glasses were refilled, and a line formed at the buffet table where a variety of hot and cold dishes were being served by the bustling guild members.

It was inevitable that she would have to speak to Sam, Meg knew, as the jostling of the crowd moved her inexorably toward him. A bevy of college girls surrounded Zach and he preened under their admiration.

Glad to escape him, Meg straightened her shoulders, lifted her chin determinedly, and walked toward Sam. She saw that he and Joan had been joined by a man with a mischievous face and a shock of graying brown hair.

"Hello, Sam," she said brightly, determined to put on the performance of a lifetime.

For a long moment, he simply stared at her, his face unreadable. Joan looked from one to the other with a puzzled frown. Meg had begun to panic, afraid he would refuse to speak to her, when Sam said quietly, "Hello, Meg."

Quickly he turned to the two people standing beside him. "Margaret Driscoll, this is Joan Gaffney, the pride of Arizona State, who will be playing Emilia in *Othello*, and Walter McGrath, who'll be Iago."

Meg acknowledged the introductions with a smile, and looked questioningly at Joan. "Arizona State?" Close up, Meg realized Joan was older than she had guessed...probably in her late thirties. She was the type Meg's father would have described as "nice looking," full-figured, tall, with green eyes and blond shoulder-length hair.

"I teach in the theater arts department there," Joan said modestly. "And work my head off in amateur theater. I'm really not in your league."

"Nonsense, Joan." Sam placed his hand over hers where it rested in the crook of his arm. "You're a marvelous actress."

Joan laughed up at him, a deep throaty laugh. Again Meg felt that unreasonable surge of jealousy. *Stop it*, she told herself. *You have no claim on Sam anymore, and he obviously has no feeling for you.*

"I can't believe Sam's the slave driver he says he is," Joan said, turning to Meg.

"Believe it!" Meg gave Sam a sidelong glance. "When do we start rehearsals?"

"Nine tomorrow morning," Sam replied, and nodded toward the brick building beyond the theater courtyard. "The offices of the festival are in that wing of the building. There'll be a bulletin board in the foyer with a schedule of rehearsal calls posted. We'll alternate times with the other plays, so check it every day. The auditorium—" he nodded toward the other end of the building "—is used for performances when it rains, and for rehearsals."

"Did you just arrive?" Joan interrupted.

"A couple of hours ago," Meg answered. "Dr. Worth didn't have time to brief me or show me around, but I suppose I'll find my way."

"I'm sure you will." Was there an undertone of meaning in Sam's words intended only for her? Meg stifled the urge to snap back at him.

She turned to Walter McGrath. "You look much too nice to play Iago."

He laughed good-naturedly. "Wait until I paste on a beard. I'll look as evil as Zach Stone."

"Walter!" Joan gave him a reproving frown, then turned to Meg with a smile. "Walt's been with the Villanova Shakespeare Repertory Theater. He's really good."

"I look forward to working with you," Meg said, warming to Walter's homely grin. "We have some great scenes together."

"Ah yes, fair lady." Walter gave a fair imitation of W. C. Fields, adding, "However, I shall perish shortly if I don't have dinner and you'll never know what you've missed."

Laughing, the four of them moved into the line at the buffet table. After filling her plate, Meg was careful to move away from Sam and Joan and begin circulating in the crowd. Walter stayed with her for a few minutes, then disappeared.

Carol came up to her, breathlessly introducing Payton James. He was an attractive man of medium height, with a trim well-muscled body. Meg found him charming and kept wondering how old he was, for his youthful face belied his thick gray hair.

As they moved away, Carol leaned to whisper in Meg's ear. "Can you find your way back to the apartments? I'm hoping to lure Payton into the dark woods and seduce him tonight."

"Carol!" Meg half laughed and stared at Carol in shocked amusement.

Carol shrugged, and in spite of the gamine grin, Meg thought she suddenly looked very vulnerable.

"I've been trying for two years, Meg, so what the heck!"

"Margaret, dear girl." Dr. Worth appeared at Meg's elbow. "This is Alexander Martin, and he's volunteered to show you around the theater complex."

"Why, that's very nice." Meg tried to cover her confusion.

"See you later then." Dr. Worth disappeared into the crowd.

Alexander Martin grinned at her. He had a nice generous mouth, Meg thought, and there was a sparkle in the depths of his gray eyes.

"Actually," he said, "I threatened to withdraw all my monetary support for the festival if I *wasn't* allowed to show you around."

"You're very kind." Meg smiled at him, well aware of the admiration in his eyes.

"Not at all," he replied with a chuckle. "I'm really very selfish." Taking her arm, he led her toward the open-air theater. The half-timbered structure was a marvelously effective reproduction of the Elizabethan Globe Theatre in London where Shakespeare's plays were originally produced.

They paused at the apron of the stage, looking up at the tiers of seats dimly seen under the starlit sky. Alex lit a cigarette. "I only wish my mother could have seen all this completed. She was a real Shakespeare buff...always flying off to some festival or other. And she was the guiding light behind this festival, although Dave Worth was the organizing genius."

"She must have been an interesting woman," Meg said, and when he nodded, asked, "You're a Shakespeare buff, too?"

"You might say that," he replied, blowing a stream of smoke into the dim theater. "I teach the seminars the festival offers twice a week."

"I didn't know about those." Meg looked at him with new respect. "Then you're a professor here at the college?"

"Oh no." His mouth curved in a warm smile. "But I do have an M.A. in English literature from Stanford. I was an assistant professor there for several years. The academic life had already palled when mother died, so I moved here to take care of her property."

They walked back up the steps onto the stage, and Alex led her down a set of stairs into a passageway connected to the basement area beneath the theater. Here were the dressing rooms with mirrored and lighted makeup tables around the walls. Alex and Meg passed the costume department where work in progress lay draped over open sewing machines and completed gowns and cloaks and pantaloons hung in colorful array on long pipe racks.

At the other side of the basement area, stairs led up to the office complex and a spacious auditorium beyond. Meg paused before the bulletin board in the foyer between offices and auditorium. Rehearsal times were already posted for the following day, beginning with Sam's at nine, Dr. Worth's *Measure for Measure* set for one-thirty, and Dr. Worth's *Comedy of Errors* at six. This was not going to be summer camp, as Carol had suggested, Meg thought wryly. It was going to be a lot of hard work. When actors weren't rehearsing the three plays, there would be costume fittings, voice coaching and dance-and-fight choreography for those whose parts demanded it.

Meg knew she would have enjoyed this kind of challenge if it wasn't for the fact that Sam's presence would keep her under constant tension. But, she reminded herself, she wouldn't see him away from the theater. Joan seemed to think she'd made a conquest. No doubt she'd keep Sam busy. Meg wished that possibility didn't hurt, wished she believed the lies she'd told herself about her feelings for Sam.

"You're very lovely." Alex's voice was low, his gray eyes watching her with unconcealed admiration.

Meg returned his look with a smile. He was very attractive himself, with all the ease of manner wealth can bring.

"I'm with another lady tonight," he continued, "but I'd very much like to see you again, soon."

"I'll be here all summer," Meg said lightly, hoping to ease the intensity she felt emanating from him.

"Yes," he agreed, and took her arm to lead her back into the courtyard.

The party was breaking up. The guild ladies had cleared the tables, and the younger members of the company had disappeared—no doubt to further partying, Meg thought with a smile. Older members of the troupe stood in little groups, talking, finishing the wine. A well-dressed woman with silver-blond hair stared meaningfully at Alex.

"Until next time," he murmured, bending to kiss Meg's hand with effortless courtesy. He walked over to join the blond woman, who glared at Meg.

Sam touched Meg's arm. "Let me walk you home." His blue eyes were grave. "I think we need to talk."

Meg shrugged. "Can you? I thought perhaps Joan had grown to your arm." When Sam's face darkened, Meg regretted her sarcasm. If only being near him didn't hurt so much. She had been so angry and bitter when she left New York she'd convinced herself her love for him was dead. She'd even managed to fool herself when she had that brief unsatisfactory affair with Rick Baldwin, one of the stars of the soap opera she'd gone to Hollywood to do. When Sam continued to phone her occasionally, she'd finally asked him to stop, knowing it would be easier to put his image from her mind if she never heard his voice.

Perhaps it was because she'd been lonely in California that the memory of the happy years with Sam drew her back. She forced herself to remember their last year, when everything fell apart. Well, if they were to work together this summer, they'd have to come to some kind of arrangement, and the sooner the better.

"Let's go." She led the way out of the courtyard, conscious of Joan's eyes following them.

"It's a beautiful campus, isn't it?" she asked as they walked along a path overhung by huge fir trees.

"Marvelous setting," Sam agreed, walking beside her, hands in his back pockets. She wished these little familiar gestures and habits of his didn't bring back such a wealth of joyous memories.

"I really envy Dave Worth," Sam went on. "He loves what he's doing, and being able to do work you love in such surroundings—"

"That sounds strange, coming from a born-and-bred New Yorker." Meg was glad Sam had begun with a safe subject.

When he answered, Sam's voice was strange and distant, with a melancholy she'd never heard from him before. "I guess there comes a time when the lights of Broadway are merely garish, and the excitement of New York seems more like frenzy."

Meg's throat clogged painfully. She longed to reach out and touch him, comfort him. But he wasn't her husband now, she reminded herself, and she forced a light tone. "That doesn't sound like the Sam Richardson of old."

"We all change." His words had such a final ring to them that they walked in silence for several minutes.

Meg looked up at the mountains towering above the town, their dark shapes silhouetted against a starlit sky. Sam was unhappy and she wished she didn't care. Determinedly she decided not to pursue it, to keep this a professional discussion.

"Zach mentioned you'd left *The Stamp Collector*," she said in a cool conversational tone.

"Well, it was a hit. Almost as big as *First Generation*." The unspoken words: *You didn't believe it would be*, hung between them. Sam cleared his throat. "I just wanted to do something else. The Guthrie Theater in Minneapolis offered me a guest directorship last March. It was an interesting experience. Regional theater is really coming into its own." After an awkward pause, he asked, "How's California?"

Lonely, she wanted to cry, but said brightly, "Great. Sunshine and smog." She didn't intend to tell him any more.

Sam broke the brief silence. "How are Ben and Ginny doing?"

"Busy as usual," Meg replied. "Dad's teaching summer school in inner-city Chicago, and you know mom. She's always caught up in the latest production at the little theater." She gave him a warm smile. "Thanks for all you did for them in New York last winter—getting tickets, dinner—"

Sam shrugged. "I was glad to. After all, they're still my friends. Anything wrong with that?"

"No," Meg answered, carefully controlling her voice. "They're both crazy about you."

His smile faded. "Sorry my family took it so badly. You know how they dote on their little Sam."

It wasn't fair, she thought, the way the Richardsons had at once cut off all contact with her. She'd thought they cared as much about her as she did them. Deep down, she supposed, her own parents blamed her for the divorce too, since they still kept in touch with Sam.

Once more they walked in silence until the lights of the apartment complex came into view. Sam cleared his throat loudly. "Well, Meg, I guess what I need to say is . . . I'm sorry if this is awkward for you. I promise you I don't intend to be difficult."

"It's all right, Sam." Meg was grateful for the darkness. Surely the pain in her heart would be reflected in her eyes. "After all, we're professionals, aren't we? You're a terrific director, you know. Any actress would give her eyeteeth to work with you."

"Professionals?" His voice was thoughtful. "That's all?"

They had walked through the breezeway into the patio area, and Meg fumbled in her purse for her key. "Thanks for walking me home," she said. "I'll see you tomorrow."

"Meg!" Suddenly his strong familiar arms were around her, the well-remembered lean body pressed against hers. "Meg," he whispered as his mouth caressed the sensitive spot beneath her ear and moved to claim her lips.

Without thought, her traitorous body responded. All the loneliness of the past year dissolved in a kiss that shook her to her depths. The familiar warmth and strength of him, the masculine scent, all possessed her in a wave of desire in which past and present were blended in one intense moment. Gently his tongue explored her mouth. Meg responded instinctively, all her being yearning toward the joy only Sam could give her.

Someone turned on a light in a nearby apartment, and Meg was shaken back into reality. With a sigh, Sam slowly released her. "Meg...love...can I come in?"

Turning away from him, Meg inserted the key in the door, her hands shaking. There had been too much pain between them, she thought wildly. Even loneliness was easier.

"No, Sam," she said harshly. "I'm not going to

bed with you." She paused, not sure of his expression in the darkness. "I don't want to be hurt again." The words were almost a cry as she slammed the door behind her.

STARING AT THE DOOR, Sam willed her to open it again, to come back into his arms and tell him she loved him, to have everything as it had once been. A door slammed somewhere inside, and the apartment was dark. His mouth tightened as all the painful memories began tumbling through his mind.

Had he thought it would be easy to win her back, or was it simply that he wanted her so much he'd convinced himself she felt the same? At first he'd tried to hold on to her by his telephone calls. But when he'd call, the conversation was stilted and desultory—except the day the divorce papers had arrived. Then he'd been hurting so badly he'd lashed out at her.

It had seemed a heaven-sent gift that day in the hospital when Harold asked him to take over at Forest Grove, then casually mentioned that Meg had been cast as Desdemona. Casually? Sam allowed himself a small smile. Harold was a friend to both of them. Even hooked up to all those tubes and electronic monitors he'd known what he was doing. He was offering Sam the second chance he'd longed for. At once Sam had canceled all his other commitments, sent back the scripts he'd been offered for summer productions, and made arrangements to come to Forest Grove.

Tonight, seeing her beautiful face in the flickering

light of the gas torches, he knew he wasn't going to let her go again. The ache in his loins intensified, recalling her passionate unthinking response to his kiss. But he realized now he couldn't push her. The waiting game might be agonizing, but it was the only way. Those divorce papers would never have his signature until he was convinced Meg no longer loved him.

THE UNFAMILIAR sound of birds singing outside her window awakened Meg. She lay still, listening, contrasting the sweet cadences with the noise of the freeway roaring past her apartment in Los Angeles. Cool morning air filled the room with the fragrance of pine and roses.

Then memory flooded back into her awakening mind, and she felt despair bubble up from deep inside. For a few minutes last night she had thought she and Sam could reach some kind of bearable truce for the summer. Then he kissed her, and she knew that desire for him still raged within her. From now on she'd be careful never to be alone with him. What did he want anyway? Did he think she was going to fall into bed with him and take care of his sexual needs for the summer?

She turned to look at her bedside clock. Nearly eight and rehearsal called for nine. She'd have to hurry.

As Meg toweled herself dry after her shower, the doorbell rang. Praying it wasn't Sam, she slipped into a robe and opened the door. Carol stood there holding a coffeepot and two mugs. She wore a bright madras shirt with her blue jeans.

"The coffee at the cafeteria is vile," Carol said with a grin. "Unless you're a big breakfast eater, I thought we could share."

"Come on in while I get dressed," Meg invited. "You're a lifesaver."

While Carol set the coffee and mugs on the gray Formica table in the little dining area, Meg hurried back to the bedroom. Pulling on a pair of straw-colored linen slacks and a dark blue Welsh fisherman's smock, Meg quickly applied the minimum of makeup she always wore offstage.

"It should be against the law to look as great as you do this early in the morning," Carol told her with a look of admiration.

Laughing, Meg twisted her dark shining hair into a loose knot, securing it with a large tortoiseshell pin. "Looks can be deceiving," she said cheerily, reaching for the mug of coffee Carol offered. No need to let Carol know how painful her awakening had been, or her struggle with the dilemma of Sam.

Morning sunlight poured through the window, casting golden squares on the gray Formica.

Keeping her tone light as they sat down at the table, Meg asked, "How did the seduction go last night?"

Carol's face clouded, and at once Meg regretted her question. After all, it was none of her business.

Resuming her casual attitude, Carol tossed her bright head. "As usual, a total failure." Shrugging, she added, "Payton thinks he's too old for me. Since his wife died eight years ago, he's devoted his life to the drama department. I know he's had plenty of other students in love with him, and he dismisses them all as schoolgirl crushes. He's cool about it, but he won't believe I'm not in the same category." Her eyes darkened with regret as she looked at Meg. Her voice was low and intense. "I really love him, Meg. The lifetime commitment kind of love. But he never lets himself go beyond a few kisses. All he can see is those years between us."

"Have you leveled with him about your feelings?" Meg asked sympathetically.

"Not really." Carol stared down into her coffee cup. Looking up at Meg, she managed a grin. "I'd feel such a fool saying 'I love you' to a man I know won't say those words back to me."

"Coward," Meg said, smiling encouragingly.

Carol looked thoughtful. "Maybe you're right. I should really confront him, but then—" she sighed deeply "—I might lose him altogether."

"Well, consider it," Meg replied, wondering how she could give advice to someone else when her own love life seemed such a failure. "Just hang in there. After all, you have all summer to work it out."

"Right!" Carol gave an exaggerated groan. "Here I am unloading on you, when I heard last night Sam Richardson is your ex-husband. That can't be too great a situation for you."

"I'll survive," Meg said briskly, feeling a prick of pain at the mention of Sam's name. She glanced at her watch. "We'd better get going. Among other things, Sam is a bear for punctuality."

While Carol rinsed the coffee mugs, Meg looked around the beige apartment. "Do you suppose we'll have time to do some shopping today? I have a feeling I won't be able to take all this beige even on a short-term basis."

Carol laughed. "The college does provide bedding and a weekly cleaning service. Too bad they didn't have an interior decorator on their staff. I bought half the green plants stocked by the local supermarket. Payton says my apartment looks like a nursery, but at least it isn't all beige."

To Meg's raised eyebrows, Carol answered, "Yes, he comes to my apartment. We aren't lovers, but we are good friends. Maybe I'll have to settle for that."

After checking the rehearsal schedule on the bulletin board, Meg and Carol made their way to the conference room where Sam was holding the first read through. Dressed in jeans and a gray sweat shirt, he was sitting at the head of a long table, making notes on a yellow legal pad, a pile of scripts beside him. Joan was seated next to him, her deep-set green eyes intent on his face. Why should that look annoy her, Meg asked herself. Sam was free and Joan had as much right to him as anyone. After one kiss could she have drifted into thinking she and Sam might get back together? Ridiculous! Meg shook off the thought.

Putting on a bright smile, she said, "Good morning, everyone."

"Good morning!" Joan's smile reminded Meg of a cat contemplating a saucer of cream.

Glancing up, Sam mumbled something. Meg wondered if he was angry about last night. Surely he wouldn't let the tension between them color his relationship with the whole cast? Sam knew his business too well for that.

Other members of the cast called greetings from where they sat around the table. Meg and Carol took their places after filling Styrofoam cups from the coffee maker standing on a side table.

"This rehearsal was called for nine o'clock," Sam said, checking his watch. "For those of you who don't know it yet, I expect everyone to be on time for rehearsal. No excuses accepted." He turned to Joan. "Will you please hand out the scripts?"

As Joan eagerly took over this chore, Sam glanced around the table. "Where the hell is Stone?" No one seemed to know, and the glowering look Sam bestowed on all of them immediately created uneasiness in the room. "He won't be late again," Sam growled.

Joan finished passing out the scripts and returned to her place. Sam continued, "While we are awaiting the late Mr. Stone, I'd like you to introduce yourselves. Give us a brief background of your experience. I've found it helps people work together if we know these things."

From old habit, Meg made sketchy notes on each one of the cast for her own future reference. She thought they looked like a good group. The ebullient Walter McGrath grinned at her. The handsome young actor who would play Cassio, the innocent soldier whom Iago makes the object of Othello's jealousy, kept staring at her.

The door swung open and Zach Stone sauntered in, wearing a white turtleneck sweater and tight jeans. His dark hair looked as though he had just come from a long session of blow drying.

"Welcome to our little group, Mr. Stone." Sam's voice was cutting.

"Good morning," Zach replied pleasantly, nodding at the group sitting around the table. He walked to the coffee maker and began filling a cup.

Meg knew Sam was seething as he watched Zach with narrowed eyes. "Will you please take your place, Mr. Stone?" he said in a barely controlled voice.

"Sure." Zach eased himself into an empty chair next to Meg.

"Now let's get this straight, Stone," Sam said icily. "No one is late to my rehearsals. Not you. Not anyone. There's no actor on earth who's irreplaceable and that includes you, Mr. Stone. If you can't be on time for rehearsal, I'll find an actor who can. Understand?" The last word rolled across the table in thunderous tones. Zach looked shocked, then petulant.

"Understand?" Sam asked again, fixing a steely glare on Zach.

Zach shrugged. "Sure."

To Meg, he looked like a child who has been chastised. The rest of the cast kept their eyes on their scripts. Meg knew none of them would ever be late again. Masterful Sam at work. "I like to be in charge," he had said to her long ago.

In spite of herself, Meg felt a little sorry for Zach. His lateness was inexcusable, but maybe Sam had resorted to overkill.

"Welcome to the world of *Othello*," Sam continued, his friendly grin encompassing the entire group. He'd put aside his curt manner and his annoyance with Zach. Now he would begin, Meg knew, to charm and cajole and demand until this cast was welded into a finely tuned unit.

To begin, Sam explained how he intended to interpret the tragic story of *Othello*. As in the old days, Meg felt the magnetism of his personality as he talked. His brilliance as a director was evident, wry asides alternating with penetrating insights. *So sure of himself*, she thought, *and so damned charming*.

He described Othello as a talented general, honored by the Venetians whose armies he had led to victory, yet never truly a part of their society because of his color; never sure of himself or his acceptance; a man of honesty and towering integrity, naive enough to believe all men shared those traits.

Meg saw that the tight-lipped Zach was scribbling notes as Sam talked. Evidently this part meant a lot to him.

Iago, Sam was explaining, is a bawdy, amoral, scheming and ambitious man, furious when Othello promotes Cassio to the position Iago covets. He is determined to find some way to revenge himself on Othello while pretending to be his friend.

As for Desdemona, she is a woman of strength and character, for she has loved and married a man outside her own race, defying society and her father to do so. She truly loves the Moor for himself, not, as he believes, for his heroic acts. Her kindness in trying to restore Cassio to the good graces of Othello after he is involved in a drunken brawl, leads to her downfall. The wily Iago sees his chance to fill the Moor with jealousy and thus destroy him.

Filled with conflicting emotions, Meg watched Sam as the read through began. Anything personal between them had to be erased from her mind. He was a damned good director, and no one knew it better than he. A demanding perfectionist, he at once began correcting the actors' reading, rewarding each one with that infectious grin of his when he was satisfied.

Everyone made copious notes from Sam's instructions as the reading continued. Meg realized she had been right about the importance of the role to Zach. His reading was much too intense, and Sam had to continually urge him to tone it down.

When Meg began the scene in act 4 with the familiar, "Willow...willow...willow..." song, Sam interrupted her. "Make an appointment with Marcia Taylor, the voice coach, Meg. You could use some help with the song."

"Sure," Meg said, an ironic twist to her mouth as she thought of all the years of singing lessons, dancing lessons, piano lessons her father had struggled to pay for. Singing had never been her strong suit, but she hadn't thought she was all that bad.

Suddenly, beneath the table, she felt Zach's knee pressing hard against hers. She almost laughed. Was he expressing sympathy or trying to come on to her? Annoyed, she wondered whether she should say something aloud, knowing it would make Zach look the fool. Reaching down, she shoved his knee away. Aware of Sam's eyes on her, she realized she had missed her cue. In her distraction, she utterly failed to give her final speech the necessary poignancy.

"This is an unhappy woman," Sam snapped. "Haven't you read the play, Meg? Let's have a little melancholy."

Furious at Zach for being the cause of her reprimand, she thought that if he tried such a thing again, he would badly need mending.

Finally, Sam called an end to the session. They would rehearse onstage tomorrow, he said. He told Meg there was a sign-up sheet on the bulletin board where she could make her voice-coaching appointment. His attitude toward her was completely businesslike. Not once did he look directly at her. He *was* angry about last night, she thought, and perhaps that was for the best. When he turned to leave, Joan was instantly at his side. Meg stood at the table, annoyed with herself for feeling forlorn as the two of them walked from the room, absorbed in their conversation.

"Let's go shopping," Carol said, appearing beside her.

Am I that transparent? Meg wondered, seeing the sympathy in Carol's eyes.

CAROL BORROWED PAYTON'S CAR for their trip to the shopping center. "It's really within walking distance, like everything else in town," she explained, "but we might have a little trouble carrying everything home."

After lunch at a hamburger stand, they made a whirlwind tour of the stores, since rehearsal for *Mea-*

sure for Measure was to begin at one-thirty. At a department store, Meg bought a persimmon-colored comforter to brighten up her bedroom; some dishes that matched the set in her apartment back in L.A.; and a minimum of pans and cutlery. She also found a persimmon-colored throw for the beige couch, added several brown-and-cream-and-gold pillows, a striped durrie rug, and a gold-and-white checked tablecloth to hide the gray Formica. At the variety store she found a small bamboo coffee table and some green plants. With a few basic groceries, she decided she and Carol could avoid the cafeteria—and the sight of Joan fawning over Sam.

At least, she thought later at the read through of *Measure for Measure*, *Carol doesn't fawn over Payton.* Playing the second female lead, Carol seemed to sense at once what Payton wanted. They had obviously learned to work as a team.

Joan did not fare as well. She was having a little trouble with her interpretation. *No wonder*, Meg allowed herself the silent catty comment. *Her character, Isabella, is supposed to defend her virtue with zeal, and Joan seems only too willing to surrender what's left of hers, if Sam asks.* Meg wished the sight of Joan didn't arouse this green-eyed monster in her. It was not that Joan was beautiful. She was wholesome looking, casual about her appearance, including the lines at the corners of her eyes. Meg chided herself that she was being petty to make something of Joan's being older than Sam.

"This is a difficult part," Payton assured Joan with a smile. He patted her hand. "We'll work on it."

Back at her apartment, Meg laid out her purchases and was pleased to see how they gave the rooms a bright pleasant air. She had made a salad and started broiling lamb chops for dinner with Carol, when the doorbell rang.

"Miss Driscoll?" A florist delivery man held out a vase filled with long-stemmed red roses. For a joyful moment, Meg thought the flowers might be a conciliatory gesture from Sam, then she remembered he'd always disliked roses because of his allergy.

Quickly opening the card, she read the bold confident script.

Beautiful lady, how do I get in touch with you, short of kidnapping?

It was signed, "Alex," with his phone number written below. In the rush of activity she had almost forgotten their encounter. Now she inhaled the fragrance of the roses, smiling as she recalled his admiring gray eyes.

"Wow!" Carol said when she arrived and Meg had shared Alex's card with her. "He's not only a marvelous-looking man, he knows how to treat a lady. Let me tell you about him. . . ."

"Carol, you're incredible," Meg declared with a laugh. "You know everything about everybody."

Giving her a hurt look, Carol replied, "I'm just interested in people." She then proceeded to tell all she had learned about Alexander Martin. His father had been a wealthy industrialist from San Francisco who fell in love with the Rockies and moved to a ranch near Forest Grove when he retired. After his death, Louise Martin, a slightly eccentric lady, not only inherited her husband's fortune, but parlayed it into another fortune by astute investment. Alex Martin, an only child, had inherited everything, and he apparently spent his life enjoying that inheritance.

"What do you think?" she asked Meg, ending her recital.

"I think he's a very nice man," Meg replied, glancing at the roses. "And I'm going to have a telephone installed."

In the glowing twilight, the two of them walked back across campus to the rehearsal of *Comedy of Errors*. They passed a young couple sitting on a bench in a grove of pine trees, locked in a passionate embrace. Meg looked away, angry with herself for immediately thinking of Sam.

The past few months she had spent in California had been busy enough to keep her mind off him for the most part. Of course, every time she called her parents they asked about Sam, with the unspoken hope that there might be a reconciliation. She tried to be fair, but it was hard not to have the complete sympathy of one's parents in this situation. She could have screamed and wept and blamed Sam to them, but she didn't because she knew they loved him. If they knew he was here, that they'd be together for the entire summer. . . .

NEXT MORNING at rehearsal, Meg found herself impressed by Zach's intensity. He was trying almost too hard, it seemed. Unbelievably, he had already memorized his long and difficult part.

When rehearsal was over, Meg quickly gathered her things and turned to leave. Unexpectedly, Sam appeared at her side as she walked out of the courtyard.

"Have lunch with me," he said with that grin she'd never been able to resist. "We'll be here together all summer. Maybe we should work out some ground rules."

Glancing at Joan, who was discussing a scene with Walter, Meg smiled impishly, forgetting her resolve to never be alone with Sam. "Sure, let's go." It pleased her to see Joan frown after them as they walked away. She looked down at her blue jeans topped by a bright pink cotton-gauze blouse, hoping they were going to eat somewhere informal.

"I've rented a car," Sam told her, steering her toward the parking lot in front of the theater. "There's a lot of beautiful country around here, and I hope to see some of it before I leave."

Slipping into her seat in the compact car, Meg noticed a picnic basket on the back seat. "Okay, Sam," she said suspiciously. "What's going on?"

"Trust me just this once." He was grinning as he drove the car onto the highway leading toward the mountains. "You can rehearse your lines while I drive if you think you're wasting your time."

Meg didn't answer as they drove out of town. Staring at the steep, pine-covered canyon walls, the incredible blue sky arching above, she miserably wished she hadn't accepted his invitation.

After several minutes of silence, Sam sighed loudly. His voice was contrite. "I remembered how much you like picnics."

For one painful instant, Meg feared she might weep as a flood of memories poured through her mind. Her eyes kept straying to Sam's strong hands holding the steering wheel. The sleeves of his blue chambray shirt were rolled back. All too well, she remembered the fair hair curling on his arms, the freckles she had found so endearing. Why was he doing this, when burned in her mind was remembrance of his angry voice on the telephone the day he'd received the divorce papers. "Get the divorce. I don't give a damn. Do you think I could go on loving someone who doesn't believe in me? I do have some pride." Too much pride, she had thought, knowing then that he no longer loved her. So why was he deliberately seeking her out now?

"Remember the time in Central Park," Sam was saying. "Just after we were married? You brought bagels and lox, and I brought champagne because I'd just gotten a play? What a picnic that was, remember?"

"I remember," Meg said in a strangled voice, not sure whether to laugh or cry, staring out the window so he wouldn't see the moisture in her eyes.

"And the time on the Manhattan ferry," he went on, "when that man's toupee blew off and landed in our potato salad?"

In spite of herself, Meg burst into laughter, remembering the hilarious scene and the poor embarrassed bald man. Before she realized what was happening, Sam had her talking about good times in New York, laughing, relaxed and enjoying herself.

Taking a hand-drawn map from his shirt pocket,

Sam consulted it, then turned off onto an unmarked dirt road. In a few minutes they rounded a hill to look down on an exquisite sapphire-blue lake set like a jewel among pine-clad mountains. Meg drew in her breath at the beauty of the scene.

"Dave was right," Sam said, stopping the car to stare out at the lake. "It was worth the drive."

They walked through a grove of aspen trees down to the lakeshore. The deep blue water shimmered with golden light in the brilliant sunshine, and lapped softly, sensuously against the rocky shore. Wild flowers dotted the grass beneath the aspens. From far down the lake came the faint hum of a fisherman's motorboat.

"It's beautiful," Meg said softly. "Thanks for bringing me, Sam."

His eyebrows arched mockingly. "And you thought I had ulterior motives!"

Meg looked away, still not sure what his motives might be. He could have, and probably should have, let well enough alone after the other night. They could meet at rehearsal and nowhere else. But incredible as it seemed, with all the hurtful past between them, she found she still enjoyed his company.

In the picnic basket she found a barbecued chicken from the supermarket, croissants, fruit and cheese and a bottle of wine.

"Very classy," she joked as they sat on the blanket he spread on the grass beneath the aspen trees. He poured the wine into wineglasses, but he'd forgotten to bring a knife for the chicken. Laughing, they tore it apart to share.

"Remember the famous scene from *Tom Jones*, where the sexual tension builds as the couple shares a meal?" Sam asked.

"So that's what you had in mind," she accused with a smile. "Forget it. Food doesn't turn me on."

"I know." Sam's voice was husky, his blue eyes intent on her face.

"Tell me about the Guthrie Theater," Meg said quickly. She mustn't get involved with him again, not on any level except the professional.

"It was a tremendous experience." Sam stared reflectively into the distance, twirling his wineglass in his long sensitive fingers. "You know, Broadway can be the most provincial place on earth. We begin to think it's the only theater there is, and that's not true. Those people in Minnesota are as aware of every subtlety in a performance as the most sophisticated Broadway audience. And their enthusiasm just pours over the footlights. I loved it." With a deprecating shrug, he added, "I hear they're looking for a permanent artistic director. I was only one of several guest directors." He fell silent.

Surprised, Meg studied his brooding face. Sam *had* changed if he was looking for something beyond Broadway. She wondered what had happened since their parting to send him in this direction. "Do you want the permanent directorship?"

"Sure," he replied with a self-conscious grin. "I want to try something new. I've finally learned there is a world beyond Broadway. But if I don't get it, something else will come along."

"Of course it will," she assured him. "Even Zach Stone admits you've made it as a director."

Sam chuckled. "Oh...Zach. I'm surprised he'd have anything good to say about me. I turned him down for the lead in *The Stamp Collector* because I felt he didn't have enough depth as an actor. He was pretty upset about it, I heard, especially when the play turned out to be a hit."

Meg decided there was no point in telling Sam her concern about Zach's overzealous attitude. "How did he get out here?" she asked offhandedly.

"He was studying with Harold Devore and Harold arranged it." He grinned at her. "I think maybe Zach took my criticism to heart and really started working at his craft."

"Speaking of working—" Meg looked at her watch "—I do have a rehearsal this afternoon."

Sam shook his head at her, an amused look on his face. "You didn't follow my instructions and read the bulletin board. Dr. James called only Joan, Zach and Walter today."

"So! You sort of pulled a fast one on me, didn't you?" Meg gave him a sideways glance, once more aware how easily they fell into a comfortable companionship. It was a feeling she'd never experienced with any other man.

"Sorry you came?" he asked, his face tense as he waited for her answer.

Surprised by his intensity, Meg gave a tremulous laugh. "No." Quickly she turned to gather the remains of their picnic into the basket. The touch of his hand on her shoulder burned through the thin material of her blouse, made her breath stop in her throat. Her heart lurched and began to pound wildly.

Gently, he pulled out her hairpin and let her hair tumble down around her shoulders. "Meg," he whispered, leaning to press his face against her hair. His warm breath touched her ear, then his lips caressed the curve between shoulder and throat. The old sweet fire rekindled, leaped into a flame spreading from the touch of his lips throughout her unforgetting body.

"Sam...don't," she murmured faintly. In reply, his strong hands cupped her face and turned her to meet his kiss. Meg felt her bones turn to water.

Sam's mouth caressed hers, teasing, arousing, until Meg moved like a moth to a flame. Her arms slowly reached to hold him, as he gently laid her back on the blanket. His kiss deepened as he drew her close against him. It was as though they had never been apart. His hand slid down her back, leaving a trail of aching fire, cupping her hips to press her against the hardness of his desire.

"Sam," she gasped, as his lips burned the hollow of her throat. That one word, meant as a protest, turned into a moan of passion.

"Sweet love," Sam whispered as his fingers slipped down the buttons of her blouse. He bent his head to let his mouth explore the hollow between her breasts.

Caught in a rising tide of emotion, Meg's fingers tangled in his sandy hair, pressing him closer. Slowly his tongue circled each bared breast, teasing at the nipples until Meg trembled with longing.

"Sam...." The name was a caress now, as waves

of desire pulsed through her blood. She felt his hand on the zipper of her jeans, stroking them away from her hips as she wiggled out of them.

With a groan, Sam bent to kiss the hollow beneath her hipbones as the jeans slid away. Gently, his fingers probed the soft moistness between her thighs, and his mouth followed, caressing, arousing her to breathless yearning.

Sighing, Meg closed her eyes against the sunlight glittering through the aspen leaves. Her eager hands reached for Sam as his lips left a trail of fire the length of her body, lingering over the sensitive spots he knew so well…below her hipbones, caressing her navel, devouring her breasts.

Reaching down, Meg unbuttoned his shirt. She drew in her breath, filled with joy as her fingers tangled in the rough mat of hair on his chest. She tossed the shirt on the grass and her arms tightened around him, luxuriating in the hard-muscled back beneath her touch.

Meg bent her head to kiss the freckles on his shoulders. Holding her, Sam watched with dark passionate eyes. Her hand followed his, enjoying the feel of his strong masculine body as she helped him push off his jeans.

Once more he drew her so close her body seemed to merge with his. His mouth claimed hers, his plundering tongue arousing her almost beyond bearing. Filled with urgent passion, Meg reached down to caress him. Sam groaned, straining her closer to him. His hands moved over her like a tantalizing flame, recalling all the secrets they'd once shared.

Meg's whole body throbbed with the yearning to be possessed. She moaned aloud in exquisite pleasure as Sam claimed her. He answered her need with his own, filling, completing her, the two of them moving together until the glitter of sunlight seemed a flame consuming them. Meg was lost in a whirlwind of rapture so devouring there was no existence beyond the passionate union of their bodies.

WRAPPED IN THE WARM GLOW of fulfillment, Meg lay curled against Sam. How had she forgotten that making love with Sam was always an adventure, never twice the same, always fulfilling? They had made love in every mood from tears to laughter, she remembered, turning to smile at him. There was no laughter in the blue eyes looking down at her now, so dark with emotion they were almost black. With tender fingers, she traced the high cheekbones of his lean face, the firm gentle outline of his lips.

Sam took her hand in his, kissing each fingertip, a gesture so dear and familiar it brought tears to Meg's eyes.

"Meg, my love," he murmured. "Nothing's changed."

Pierced by pain, Meg turned her face against his shoulder. In a strangled voice, she said, "No, nothing's changed," knowing that although they spoke the same words, their meanings were diametrically opposed. The passion they shared had not resolved their differences. Their bodies had always been incredibly in tune, but they had not shared what was locked in their hearts. *If only. .if only. . .* she thought, wanting with all her being to make it right again, to have things as they once were.

Sam gently brushed back her hair, his tongue teasing at her ear. Instinctively, Meg lifted her face to his and gave herself completely to his kiss.

Letting out his breath in a long sigh, Sam lay back, pillowing her head on his shoulder. Far away, a fisherman's motor coughed, coughed again, then died. A breeze rustled through the aspen trees, blowing off the icy lake. Meg shivered and turned to look at her watch.

Leaning on her elbow, she looked down into Sam's face. "I have an appointment with the voice coach at four." She kissed the tip of his nose.

"Plenty of time." He gave her a lazy smile, his eyes devouring her face.

She didn't want it to end, this languorous moment of utter contentment. They seemed suspended in time and space, lost to the past and the future. There was only now, and the strong arms drawing her close, his mouth seeking hers. Closing her eyes, Meg gave herself to the warmth of his embeace, trying to shut out the knowledge that she had responsibilities back in Forest Grove.

With a sigh she drew away, holding his face softly between her palms, gazing lovingly into his eyes.

"We'd really better get started back, Sam."

"Bubble burster!" he said, laughing and pulling her back into his arms.

Even as she responded to his kiss, Meg felt the old bitter brew of anger and resentment churning inside. If only he hadn't used those words—the words he'd so often used to end her discussions about the realities of life. "Don't burst my bubble," he'd say, "Ms Bubble Burster." She remembered long ago screaming at him, "Don't call me that!" But he had thought it a joke. Damn him! Too insensitive to understand that the words were a reproach to her.

Pushing him away, Meg hastily began to dress. Sam watched in silence, then reached out to gently stroke her hair. "Meg," he said softly. "Can't we start over?"

Bitterness welled up in her, tinging her voice. "It still won't work, Sam. Like you said, nothing's really changed. I'm still the bubble burster, the reality freak who worries about paying the bills, or using other people's money."

Her voice trailed off as she saw anger blaze in Sam's face. "Damn!" he said, and started pulling on his clothes. "There are two words you don't know the meaning of—trust and faith. And you'd never listen to explanations, not about dad's money, or about Linda, or anything else."

Standing up, Meg looked down at him. For a moment the pain in his eyes almost destroyed her resolve. Tearing her eyes away, she picked up the picnic basket.

"Let's just forget this afternoon ever happened," she said far too loudly over the roaring pain in her mind. And she turned to walk toward the car.

5

WALKING WITH CAROL through the cool pine-scented morning, Meg tried to shake her depression. Memory of the passion she had shared with Sam beside the lake yesterday surged through her. All night she had tossed, sleepless, trying to wipe the incredible joy of those moments from her mind.

She must stop thinking about Sam. All those bonds were severed. Tightening her lips resolutely, Meg told herself that she was doing work she loved, in a magnificent setting. It was only sensible to set aside personal problems.

From beside her, Carol asked, "Everything okay, Meg?"

Glancing at her friend, Meg smiled, admiring the petite figure clad in blue jeans and a yellow University of Washington sweat shirt. "Sure," she replied. She was wearing blue jeans too, with a light blue polo shirt, a white sweater tied around her shoulders against the morning chill. "Beautiful morning, isn't it?" She made her voice sound jaunty.

"Yeah." Carol gave her a doubtful frown as they entered the theater.

Morning sun filtered through the pine trees onto the stage. The dark red seats were still damp with dew. A bustle of beginning rehearsal, the buzz of voices, filled the small arena.

Put on your acting face—quickly, Meg told herself as her eyes were inevitably drawn to Sam. He was leaning against the stage, going over the script with Joan. The sight of his long lean body shook Meg with such a wave of desire she was sure it must be visible.

Struggling to control her feelings and put away the memory of yesterday, Meg opened her script. After the silent ride back from the lake, she had curtly refused Sam's tentative invitation to dinner, slammed out of his car and hurried into her session with the voice coach.

"If we were in New York, that would be called an 'item,'" a supercilious voice said. Zach had appeared beside her, nodding toward Sam and Joan. "They've been inseparable since they arrived."

Suppressing a wild impulse to slap him, Meg frowned. Zach seemed to take perverse pleasure in jabbing at her wounds. At least, he never missed an opportunity to point out Sam's apparent interest in Joan.

"What's the matter, Zach?" she flared at him. "Is Joan the only female you haven't been able to add to your harem?"

Her gibe brought a look of surprise to Zach's handsome features. Then he grinned complacently. Determined to end the conversation, Meg quickly walked over to speak to Walter McGrath.

Rehearsal went smoothly. Sam was brisk and businesslike. Never did he allow his eyes to meet Meg's. Concentrating fiercely on her lines, Meg buried her emotions in the back of her mind. Only once did she lose her immersion in the character. Walter and Joan were doing a scene as Iago and Emilia, husband and wife involved in a quarrel. Meg glanced covertly at Sam watching his actors, making notes in that wild handwriting of his. *Oh, Sam,* the words rose painfully in her mind. *Why do we keep hurting each other? It should be over. I shouldn't care anymore.* Their differences were irreconcilable, and there could be no return to the status quo. So why couldn't they walk away and forget it?

Meg was suddenly distracted by a low murmur of voices.

The members of the cast not on stage made up their audience. Everyone had turned to look at the florist delivery man who had just walked into the theater carrying a huge box.

"For God's sake!" Sam stood up and glared at the man. "There's a rehearsal going on here. No interruptions allowed."

"Sorry, sir." The man looked embarrassed. "But I have orders to deliver these to Miss Driscoll at this time."

"Meg!" Sam glowered at her. "Take care of it."

Meg took the box and signed for it. She intended to leave it there and return to finish the scene, but Carol called eagerly, "Open it, Meg." The other members of the cast added their urging, and Meg complied.

Three dozen long-stemmed red roses lay in dewy perfection on the green florist paper.

"Who sent them?" Carol asked with seeming in-

nocence. Meg shot her a sharp look. They both knew
it must be Alex Martin.

His card, written in a bold confident script, read:

Lovely lady, please have dinner with me tonight. I'll be waiting for your call.

                                        Alex

Again he gave his telephone number. Meg quickly
slipped the note into her jeans pocket.

"They're from Mr. Martin," she told the cast, who
replied with a chorus of "Ahs!" rendered in significant tones.

Meg laughed, not daring to look at Sam. "Forget
it, you gossip mongers," she said gaily. In spite of
herself, she was inordinately pleased by Alex's extra-
vagance.

Sam's eyes glinted with anger, and his voice was
sharp. "Well, I guess this breaks up rehearsal for today. Same time tomorrow. Don't forget next week
we'll be rehearsing afternoons, and the week after, in
the evenings."

As he began gathering up his scripts and notes,
Meg said apologetically, "Sorry, Sam."

"Sure," he replied, not looking at her. His eyes
were on the box of roses and his jaw tightened.
"Long-stemmed red roses," he said in a derisive tone.
"Shows a lot of imagination, doesn't he?"

Don't ruin this for me, Meg wanted to say, and
glared at him. When his eyes met hers, she saw in
their blue depths an anguished mixture of pain and
anger. *Violets*, something said in the back of her

mind. It was always violets Sam sent. No matter how hard up they were, he managed to scrounge enough money to send violets for each of her opening nights. The remembered scent of them overwhelmed her for a moment. *Like the violets*, he'd said, *there's more to you than meets the eye*. Deep in her being something wanted to toss out the roses and fling herself into Sam's arms. But he had already started out of the theater.

Damn you, Meg stared after him. *I'll get you out of my system yet, Sam Richardson . . . and Alex Martin may be just the man to do it!*

THE BLUE MERCEDES 450SL purred smoothly down the long poplar-lined lane toward a low adobe ranch house surrounded by pine and oak trees. Glancing sideways at Alex, Meg couldn't imagine he'd ever driven anything but an imported sports car. He wore an impeccably tailored camel's hair jacket with his navy slacks. His smooth-shaven face was attractively tanned, slim and aristocratic.

Looking out the car window, Meg saw that the size of his home was impressive. Painted white fences enclosed the pastures where thoroughbred horses frolicked in the late-afternoon sunlight. The sun, just setting over the distant western hills, laid long shadows across the lawns and pastures.

It's like a scene from one of those glossy high-society magazines showing how the "other half" lives, Meg mused.

"Did I remember to tell you how lovely you look?" Alex asked.

Meg smiled. "Several times." She was aware of how the simple tangerine-colored silk dress set off her dark hair and olive complexion. Despite her model's objective awareness of her beauty, it pleased her that this intelligent and sophisticated man seemed so enthralled by her looks.

Tonight she had every intention of putting Sam from her mind and enjoying Alex's company. Perhaps he would make it easier to finally purge her heart of Sam Richardson.

A smiling Oriental houseboy in a crisp white shirt and dark trousers opened the door for them.

"This is Kim," Alex said. "He keeps my house in order and his wife, Mai, is the world's greatest cook." Kim smiled and bowed. Alex took Meg's hand in his. "We'll have drinks on the terrace, Kim. The usual for me, and for Miss Driscoll. . . ." He looked questioningly at Meg.

"White wine, please," she answered, looking around the huge living room off the entry. Heavy Navaho rugs lay on the polished tile floors, dark Spanish-style furniture was upholstered in rough white Haitiian cotton. A huge adobe fireplace filled one wall. Beside it, a bookcase held a collection of colorful kachina dolls.

Alex paused to flip on the stereo, then led her out onto the tile-paved terrace, which seemed an extension of the living room. The swimming pool, surrounded by elegant wrought-iron lawn furniture, gleamed soft turquoise in the failing light. Green lawns and carefully tended flower beds were displayed beyond it, and beyond that, wide pastures gave way to a splendid view of the mountains.

"This is a lovely place," Meg told him as he seated her in a chair beside a glass-topped table.

"Glad you like it." With a smile, he added, "I guess it's not too bad for bachelor digs." His gray eyes were warm as he stood looking down at her.

"I can't imagine why a man as charming as you is still a bachelor." Meg smiled up at him.

Alex looked pleased as Kim appeared with drinks on a silver tray. Handing her the glass of wine, Alex took his martini.

"I don't mean to misinform you." He sat down opposite her. "Perhaps bachelor is the wrong word. I'm divorced."

"Oh," she said, thinking, *So am I and half the rest of the world.*

"When I decided to come here to live," he continued, "my wife refused to join me. She had what she considered an exciting career in San Francisco and—" his mouth twisted wryly "—she wasn't willing to give it up to be with me."

"That must have been difficult," Meg murmured.

He shrugged. "It wasn't a tragedy. At that point, we really had very little in common, anyway." Lifting his glass in a brief salute, he drank, watching her over the rim of his martini. "I rather like my life here, although some might think it aimless."

"The role of country gentleman seems to suit you very well." Meg leaned back in her chair, smiling at him.

Alex lit a cigarette. "I have to admit it palls occasionally. That's why I usually winter abroad, in the south of France or somewhere like that."

"With the rest of the jet set," Meg teased.

Alex chuckled. "I don't aspire to the jet set. I just don't like to spend the winter shivering in the snow."

Meg took one of the hot crab puffs Kim offered, thinking Alex's life sounded ideal. Everything arranged, the paths all smoothed, no shivering in the snow, no worrying about paying the rent. With a suppressed sigh of envy, she thought she might like to try such a life, one with no struggles, doing only as one pleased.

The fresh rainbow trout almandine was elegantly served in the dining room, on thinnest Haviland china. It was accompanied by a crisp dry Moselle wine. The meal ended with a delicious sorbet made, Alex told her, from the wild raspberries that grew in the mountains above the town.

It was evident that Alex had played host often and knew how to entertain. His conversation was light, witty and well informed. Relaxed, amused by his company, Meg realized it had been a long time since she'd enjoyed an evening so much. No wonder Nedra, the blond woman at the party, had glared at her so. One could become accustomed to this kind of life and this kind of attentive treatment. Who would wish to see a rival come on the scene?

While Kim served brandy and coffee on the terrace, Alex switched the stereo to a collection of Big Band Era tunes. With the soft music flowing around her, Meg leaned back in the cushioned chair. The pool gleamed in the rising moon, the mountains outlined beyond it.

She sighed as Alex handed her a baccarat brandy glass. "I could learn to like this Sybaritic life."

His gray eyes darkened as they looked into hers. "I hope you will," he said softly.

Before she could summon a reply to that surprising statement, he took her hand and drew her into his arms. "Big Band tunes always bring out the dancer in me," he said lightly.

"Mmm...yes." Meg followed his expert guidance as they moved together across the tile floor of the terrace. His arm tightened around her waist, pressing her close against him. She felt the pressure of his lips against her hair as the two of them swayed gently together.

Meg felt a sudden rush of panic. She wanted to say, *Don't rush me, please Alex. My wounds are too deep.*

The old hurts throbbed painfully as there flashed through her mind a picture of Sam and her dancing...where? Yes...at his sister's wedding...a hotel ballroom filled with laughter and good wishes. Sam's arms were around her, their bodies moving together to the rhythm of the music, knowing the love between them was almost tangible. Then she was smiling up at her own father as he led her diligently through a fox trot, a waltz with Sam's dad, and gratefully, back into the loved familiar arms, her body moving as one with Sam's.

Alex paused, the sensuous sounds of old love songs weaving a web around them in the moonlight. Cupping her face in one hand, he bent to touch her lips.

"You're incredibly beautiful," he murmured. "Moonlight becomes you, just as the old song says." His arms tightened, holding her close as his lips claimed hers, gently at first, slowly growing more urgent in their demands.

Wanting to respond to him, Meg was surprised at how cold she felt. She *wanted* to feel something. Alex was charming and wonderful, and she felt absolutely nothing. Gently, she pushed him away.

"It's been a marvelous evening, Alex, but I'd better get back. I've an early rehearsal tomorrow to make up for the one I missed tonight." She saw his struggle to conceal his disappointment.

"I don't mean to rush you, Meg." He caressed her cheek with the palm of his hand. "I find you quite irresistible, you know."

"And so are you," she replied with a light laugh, squeezing his hands. With an exaggerated sigh, she added, "Ah, the sacrifices an actress makes for her art."

Alex gave a soft amused chuckle. "All right, beautiful Meg. But we will have other evenings like this, won't we?"

"I certainly hope so," and she reached up to kiss his cheek. "It's been absolutely heavenly."

As THEY PASSED the trellis of climbing roses separating the apartment complex from the street, Meg impulsively picked one of the blossoms. Handing it to Alex, she said in a teasing voice, "A small token, in return for all the extravagant roses you've showered on me."

"Only the beginning," he told her in an assured voice, his eyes gleaming with pleasure as he held the blossom to his nose.

Meg had a feeling he intended to kiss her, but the sound of voices from the apartment patio deterred him. Four people were seated there in the shadows where moonlight filtered through the oak trees.

"Here's Meg!" Carol cried, and waved at her. "And Mr. Martin. Hi!"

"Hi," Alex replied, obviously nonplussed to be greeted in such a manner.

Payton smiled and nodded beside Carol.

"Would you believe we're sitting here talking Shakespeare?" Joan asked.

Sam pushed back his chair. The sight of Meg with another man was akin to swallowing a pan of red-hot coals. He wanted to do something terrible and desperate...snatch her and spirit her away...something wild and improbable. Jealousy was not an emotion he'd had much experience with, and it seized him like a fevered sickness. Like the time he'd called her in L.A. and a male voice answered. God, he'd been ready to kill, until the sound of other voices in the background confirmed Meg's statement that there was a party going on.

"William Shakespeare was the greatest writer the world has ever known," Alex said jovially, making conversation.

"An Elizabethan hack writer," Sam replied in a cutting voice. He felt a vindictive satisfaction when he saw Alex bristle at the words.

"That's a ridiculous statement," Alex said coolly, "to make about a writer of unquestioned genius."

"Of course he was a genius," Sam answered quickly, knowing he was baiting Alex for unworthy reasons. "Some of his work is magnificent. But many of his plays were written to order, put together so quickly that real craft is lacking."

Meg's voice was tight with an unspoken warning. "We used to discuss this in Harold Devore's class, but I don't think we're on that level now."

"I tend to agree with Sam," Payton spoke easily. "Every Shakespearean director I've worked with has had to rewrite his stage directions, if nothing else. In *Measure for Measure*, for example, he even has Claudio's beloved Juliet onstage in one scene, saying nothing and serving no purpose whatsoever."

Sam made no effort to hide his triumphant grin at Alex's obvious annoyance. Meg shot him an icy glance as she took Alex's hand and the two of them walked toward the entrance to the patio.

"Good night, all," Alex called over his shoulder, politely formal but failing to conceal his annoyance. He looked down at Meg, then glanced uneasily at the others who were trying to pretend they weren't watching.

Working hard to mask his feelings, Sam watched them, knowing Alex would have preferred to be alone, to kiss Meg good-night. At the thought of her in another man's arms, he made a faint sound of pain. Right now he didn't feel particularly proud of himself. He'd challenged Alex like a gladiator seeking a duel. Shifting uncomfortably in his chair, Sam knew he'd behaved abominably, and he also knew an apology would only make things worse.

As Meg returned, Sam tried to catch her eye, but she refused to look at him. Of course she was furious with him. He'd blown it again.

Joan rose from the table, picking up a sheaf of papers lying there. "I'll edit these pages tonight, Sam. So far, I think you've got something really good going."

"Sam's writing a play." Carol turned to Meg. "Joan read a scene for us."

"Sounds like a winner," Payton added.

"I teach playwriting at Arizona State," Joan said, smiling at Meg. "Sam thought I might know something he doesn't. But I think he's pretty much got it under control."

In his present state of despair, Sam could find no pleasure in Joan's praise. Meg gave him a surprised look.

"I didn't know you were writing a play." Her laugh sounded forced. There were glints of anger in her eyes as they met his. "You always said you could write something better than most of the scripts you saw, but I didn't think you'd ever have the nerve to try it."

Good shot, Sam thought. He gave her a dark look. "That was a basic problem," he said in a flat voice. "You never really had faith in me."

An uncomfortable silence fell. Sam could have kicked himself when he saw the hurt expression in her eyes, quickly suppressed. *I've really made an ass of myself tonight*, he thought. *Airing our dirty laundry in public.*

Meg turned away, saying a clipped, "Good night." As she unlocked the door to her apartment, Sam watched, overwhelmed by longing. She closed the door behind her, never looking back.

Sam sat very still, almost unaware of the embarrassed good-nights the others were saying. In all his life he had never felt so alone.

MEG STOOD for a moment, leaning back against the closed door, shaking with suppressed emotion. She had never known Sam to behave so badly. His whole attitude toward Alex was uncalled for. After all, Alex had only been making polite conversation. Could Sam be jealous? It seemed improbable, but nothing else explained such behavior. The idea wormed its way into her consciousness...Sam...jealous. Unexpectedly, she felt lighthearted, knowing that if it was true it meant he still cared for her.

But not on the old terms! Meg remembered how he had said, "You never really had faith in me." Sighing, she put the chain on the door and went into the bedroom. They'd been caught up in a riptide, drawn farther and farther apart. There seemed little possibility they could ever reach the calm shore of love again.

6

SPRING RIPENED INTO SUMMER as the weeks of rehearsal passed. Only the years of training and discipline made those weeks bearable for Meg. In spite of the underlying tension of Sam's presence, she managed to throw herself into the frenzied activity of constant rehearsal, costume fittings and voice coaching.

With roses arriving every week and the Mercedes picking Meg up, it was inevitable there would be gossip in the company. Meg was aware of it. Carol teased her about her ardent admirer. What no one knew was that Alex would have preferred to see her every night. She pleaded the demands of night rehearsals and early-morning calls, limiting their dates to once a week. Unwillingly she admitted to herself that fending off Alex's advances could be wearing. Although she was content to let the relationship remain platonic, he gave every indication that was not his intention.

One afternoon, with less than two weeks of rehearsal time left, Meg gathered up her scripts and purse as work on *Measure for Measure* ended. Looking around for Carol, she spotted her with Payton onstage. They were studying the script lying on a table, Payton's fingers gently caressing the nape of Carol's neck. Smiling to herself, Meg silently cheered Carol's progress.

"Bye, you two," she called. "I have a wardrobe fitting."

Downstairs, Sam was waiting at the wardrobe department. His tall lean frame lounged against the wall, his eyes raking her as she came down the corridor.

With a sigh of resignation, Meg thought she might have guessed he'd be there. Thorough director that he was, Sam would insist on approving her costumes for Desdemona. The past weeks she had contrived never to be alone with him. In the presence of others she could keep her emotions under control. The wardrobe mistress would be with them, but just the same she wished he hadn't come.

"Hi, Sam," she said gaily. "Ready for the fashion show?"

"Mrs. Martelli hasn't arrived," he replied, staring at her in a disconcerting manner. Then he grinned that damned endearing grin of his. Meg felt her heart flip-flop and her pulse quicken, as she responded to the irresistible physical attraction he still had for her.

"But I have the keys," he added, producing them and unlocking the door. He switched on the overhead lights.

Hoping Mrs. Martelli would arrive promptly, Meg walked into the room. Avoiding Sam's penetrating gaze, she searched for her costumes. Desdemona was to wear two gowns, changing for the second act when she arrives in Cyprus to join her husband. The last change of costume would be a nightdress for the murder scene. Unable to recognize her gowns, Meg checked the tags attached to two costumes on dress forms. "Desdemona, act 1, Desdemona, act 2," she read aloud with a frown. Looking up, she met Sam's piercing look. "These aren't like the sketches I saw," she said in an annoyed voice. "They both had an Elizabethan ruff."

"Harold's idea," Sam replied with a quirk of his mouth. "I saw the damned things. Do you think I'm going to let you cover that gorgeous throat of yours with a ruff? I asked the designer for mid-seventeenth century styles. They're more becoming to everyone."

His high-handed manner infuriated her. Even though she had to admit the richly embroidered, heavy costumes would be more comfortable with low scoop necklines, he had no right to change them without consulting her.

"You've become a real tyrant, Mr. Richardson," she said in a tight voice. She had meant to sound amused, but it didn't come out that way.

"Psychologists call it sublimating." The words might have been one of his old joking asides, but his tone failed him just as hers had done. Sam's face was grim.

"Sublimating what?" she asked lightly, under control now and determined to change the mood of the conversation.

"A lot of anger." He stared into her face. "And one hell of a lot of rejection."

Still struggling to change the direction of this exchange, Meg gave an unconvincing laugh. "I didn't know the great Sam Richardson ever met with rejection."

"You know damn well what I mean." Seizing her by the shoulders, he drew her toward him.

Suddenly tender, he cupped her chin in his strong fingers, bending to claim her lips. She could no more resist his touch than a sunflower could resist turning to the sun. His tongue teased at her mouth until she opened to him, giving herself blindly as his kiss deepened. Lost in the rising heat of her own passion, Meg finally heard someone coughing loudly near the door.

Quickly, she stepped away from Sam. His hands released her reluctantly as they turned to face the embarrassed Mrs. Martelli.

After they exchanged pleasantries with the wardrobe mistress, Meg went behind a screen to change. She'd never be free of him, she thought miserably, as Mrs. Martelli zipped her costume. She couldn't help responding to his touch. She just mustn't ever see him again after this summer. Never see Sam again . . . the thought devastated her now as completely as it had a year ago on an airliner bound for Los Angeles.

A few minor adjustments were made, along with Mrs. Martelli's observation that the lower necklines Sam had ordered were much more flattering.

"What about the nightgown?" Sam asked, lounging in a chair at the end of the cutting table.

Meg shrugged. "A nightgown is a nightgown." His reply was a significant look, and she flushed, remembering how seldom she'd worn a nightgown when they were together.

Looking away, she wondered how soon the whole company would know Sam had been kissing her in the wardrobe department. He had shown not the slightest trace of embarrassment, merely sat down and observed her costumes with an amused smile.

"I know a little about nightgowns." Sam was watching her closely, his smile widening into a grin, his eyebrows raised.

Indeed, Meg thought, feeling her flush deepen. There had been a sexy black satin-and-lace number he'd given her for Christmas one year. She'd modeled it for him, and it had lain all night on the floor beside their bed.

"That thing you agreed on looked like something Queen Victoria might have worn," he continued. Turning to Mrs. Martelli, Sam asked, "Did you finish the gown we discussed?"

"Yes, Mr. Richardson." She reached for the white material on the sewing machine. "I had a hard time finding exactly what you wanted." She held the gown against her ample figure.

"Beautiful." Sam nodded at Meg. "Try it on for me."

Taking the gown from Mrs. Martelli, Meg held up the flowing diaphanous material, then turned furiously on Sam. "What makes you think I'll wear this onstage?" She held it to the light. "It's transparent."

Sam shrugged. "So what?"

"Excuse me," Meg replied coldly. "I was under the impression we were doing Shakespeare, not a Las Vegas nightclub act."

Frowning at her, Sam used a patient tone as

though speaking to a child. "Remember the scene, Meg. In a jealous rage, Othello murders his adored wife." In a voice only she could hear, he added, "That's a scene I could play without any rehearsal."

Surprised at his vehemence, Meg stared at him. Finally she said in a shaky voice, "I'm not your wife, Sam."

It seemed to her a flash of pain crossed his face as he quickly looked away. After a moment, he growled, "Wear a body stocking under it, then. After all, this woman is trying to win back her husband. She's not going to be wearing a wool wrapper."

Pretending she hadn't heard a word, Mrs. Martelli quickly fitted the flowing gown to Meg and agreed to order a body stocking in Meg's size. When Sam thanked her, she merely nodded and busied herself with the costumes, avoiding their eyes.

"Truce?" Sam turned to Meg with a grin.

Damn you, she thought resentfully. *I keep trying to cut you out of my heart, and you keep drawing me back. Surely you know, as I do, that it will never work. I was always second fiddle to you and I'm not going to be second again. At least I'm first with myself now.* That thought brought no comfort, for she knew that the moment she'd left Sam she'd regretted it. Now there was no going back.

Caught up in her thoughts, Meg did not reply. Sam touched her shoulder gently. "Have dinner with me, Meg?"

"Sorry." Meg summoned her coldest tone of voice. "I'm having dinner with Alex."

As though burned, Sam's hand jerked away from

her shoulder. Without looking directly at him, she knew the struggle he had to conceal his emotions. His voice carried a bitter note.

"Just what is the relationship between you and Alexander the Great?"

Picking up her purse and scripts, Meg tossed her head. "It's none of your business, Sam. Why do I have to keep reminding you I'm no longer your wife?"

When he replied in a low emotional voice, "Because I don't want to believe it," Meg fled from the room, half-blinded by tears.

THE RESTAURANT was located in a restored Victorian mansion in the older section of town. Lace curtains, oak dining tables and sideboards, costumed waitresses, all created a pleasant timeless ambience that Meg found relaxing.

"You seem pensive tonight," Alex said, smiling at her across their secluded table in a bay-windowed nook. "Anything wrong?"

"Just one of those days," Meg replied. Her encounter with Sam had left her shaken. She kept thinking she'd let go of all emotion connecting the two of them, then find it wasn't true. Objectively she knew there could never be anything between them again, even though the old chemistry still existed. She assured herself that, away from his physical presence, she could survive very well. Maybe even forget him.

"What you need," Alex told her with a winning smile, as he poured the ruby-hued cabernet into her glass, "is to get away from it all."

"With opening night less than two weeks away?" Meg laughed. "Things get more frenzied by the day. I was lucky I wasn't called to rehearse tonight, so I could have dinner with you."

"I must speak to Dave Worth about his slave-driving tactics." Alex gazed at her fondly. "You're much too beautiful to live this hectic kind of life."

"But I rather like it," Meg protested mildly, watching the waitress serve a rich brown sauerbraten with sweet-and-sour red cabbage.

"There are life-styles you haven't tried yet, my dear." His hand covered hers as he looked deep into her eyes. "I could show you the world."

She said in a teasing voice, "If you keep feeding me like this, you wouldn't want the world to see me."

He chuckled. "This place is known for its German food. I intend to ply you with their marvelous fresh-strawberry torte, too."

"Delicious." Meg tasted the meat. "Ah well, eat, drink and be merry, for tomorrow we diet."

"That's the least of your worries." His eyes were admiring. "Mine, at the moment, is how to wangle a day off for you. You're looking tired. How about going to my cabin at the lake on Sunday?"

"Rehearsal—" Meg began.

"Forest Grove has blue laws," Alex said with mock sternness. "Everything is supposed to shut down on Sunday. You know there are no performances on Sunday, so why should rehearsal be held on Sunday?"

"Your reasoning is illogical," Meg replied with a laugh. "But I like it."

"Then you'll go?"

Why not? she thought. Why not, for this brief summer interlude, let Alex show her his world. Her own wasn't all that pleasant at the moment. This man was handsome, attentive and interesting. When she was with him, she could almost put Sam out of her mind. "Why not?"

IT RAINED ON SUNDAY. Black clouds hung over the mountaintops as the Mercedes wound up the steep canyon road. Lightning flashed, thunder roared, and an increased tempo of rain splashed against the windshield. Lulled by the monotonous sweep of the wipers, Meg leaned back in the soft glove-leather seat. She glanced at Alex. He drove with easy assurance, the way he did everything else. His aristocratic profile was outlined against the rain-streaked window. Not handsome like Zach or rugged like Sam, he was still a terribly attractive man. Perhaps it was his ease of manner that made him so engaging.

By the time they had passed the south shore of the lake, looking down on its dark blue waters from a pine-studded cliff, the rain had dwindled to a patter.

At the western end of the lake, Alex paused to open the gate to a private driveway. The storm clouds had broken up, drifting quickly away. Wisps of cloud trailed among the forested mountaintops, as soft as cotton wool.

High above them, Meg caught a glimpse of a log house with a deck overlooking the lake. It seemed to have grown there as naturally as the pine trees.

"This was one of the first cabins built at the lake,"

Alex told her as he drove the Mercedes beside the house and parked it. "I've remodeled it since I bought it."

"Of course," Meg agreed a bit ironically, for the cabin was very large and well-cared for. She followed Alex up the steps to the deck and looked around as he unlocked the door. Thick pine forest blanketed the hills below, nearly to the lakeshore where green meadows appeared. The new-washed meadows gleamed and the lake glittered in the sunlight.

"It's a beautiful setting," she told him as he led her into a living room furnished with antique rustic furniture, a rock fireplace filling one wall.

"One of my favorite hideaways," Alex said with a smile. He set the picnic basket on the counter in the well-equipped modern kitchen, and began opening a bottle of wine.

After a quick tour of the cabin, they settled in cushioned willow chairs on the broad deck overlooking the lake. Alex poured the white wine. "Here you are," he said, handing her a glass. "Now you should have nothing on your mind except the fantastic view—and me."

"The view is spectacular," she agreed, sipping her wine.

"And me?"

For the briefest of moments, she hesitated, wondering what response he sought with that leading question. Smiling, she replied, "You are the perfect host."

"Host wasn't exactly the word I was looking for."

A slight frown creased his forehead between dark brows. Then he shrugged. "If that's to be my role, would *madame* care to have lunch served out-doors?"

As she joined him in setting the lunch of melon and prosciutto on the varnished wicker table, Meg wondered for the first time about Alex's motives. He was obviously used to flattery and liked it. Perhaps he had chosen her to provide a summer's amusement for himself. It was an unworthy thought, she chided herself. He had been the soul of gracious behavior, never pressing his demands beyond what she indicated she desired. Just enjoy, Meg told herself as they sat down to their meal.

Refilling her wineglass, Alex spoke in a matter-of-fact tone. "I understand you and Sam Richardson were once married."

Of course he'd have heard, but Meg didn't want to share her feelings about Sam with anyone. Carefully controlling her voice, she said, "Our relationship is strictly professional now."

His serene gray eyes regarded her with real concern. "That's undoubtedly why he's so critical and demanding of you. I can speak to him about it if it bothers you. After all, I am president of the board."

With a rueful smile, Meg imagined Sam exploding if Alex interfered. "Dear Alex . . . no," she said, reaching across the table to squeeze his hand. "Sam's the director and I'm the actress. He treats me like any other member of the cast."

Giving her a doubtful look Alex shrugged. "If you say so." After a brief silence in which he served a dessert of pale green grapes, Camembert cheese and crackers, Alex asked, "What will you do when the season ends?"

"Go back to L.A., I suppose," Meg replied, hating to even think of her uncertain future while she was sitting in this luxurious spot.

"What if you had another choice?" He smiled mysteriously.

Meg laughed. "I'm a working girl, Alex. I don't have a lot of choices."

Leaning back in his chair, Alex sipped his wine, his gray eyes regarding her intently. "I've just made arrangements to rent a condo on Mykonos for a month this fall. The Greek islands are fabulous after the tourists go home, and the Aegean Sea has to be seen to be believed." He paused. "There is nothing in the world like Homer's 'wine-dark' sea."

Meg sighed, a bit envious, wondering whether the fabled Greek islands would be forever beyond her reach.

"Then I plan to be at my pied-à-terre in San Francisco for the opera season. Do you like opera?"

"I adore it," she replied, then laughed. "I guess I like anything that's performed onstage."

Alex's gray eyes darkened, his voice was low and husky. "It would be marvelous to share all that with you."

Meg caught her breath, her mind filled with pictures of the dark blue sea, the white houses and windmills of Mykonos. How wonderful to live like that, with the whole world open to you. It was tempting beyond belief, and yet— She knew Alex wasn't speaking of marriage. Even if their relationship had progressed that far, she knew that a man who moved constantly, as he did, from one interest to another, must make only brief commitments.

She became aware that he was watching her intently. Slowly he began to smile. "I'm rushing you, beautiful Meg. But you must know you've captivated me. Perhaps by the end of the season, I can have captured you, also."

Meg laughed nervously. "Perhaps." Seeing the depth of feeling in his eyes, she added, "Please don't stop trying."

Alex took her hand and kissed it softly. Standing, he drew her up into his arms. His kiss, gentle at first, grew more insistent, his tongue flicking against her lips, his arms pressing her close against him. Closing her eyes, Meg leaned into his embrace, wanting to feel the flame of desire leap into life. It was pleasant, nothing more. Gently she disengaged herself from his embrace, and kissed his chin to placate the disappointment in his face.

Turning, she strolled toward the telescope mounted on the deck. "Do you spy on your neighbors?" she asked, teasing.

Alex looked amused. "There are always the stars at night. And at one time I was an avid bird-watcher. Those meadows teem with migrating fowl in the autumn."

Bending her head to the eyepiece, Meg adjusted the focus. She stifled the soft exclamation that rose in her throat. Her eyes stung. Fate was against her, or why would the telescope at once pick up the fallen log where she had shared lunch with Sam, the grass beneath the aspens where they had made love. A pain clutched at her throat. Blindly, she turned from the telescope to find Alex's arms waiting for her.

7

THE SHRILLING of the telephone awakened Meg. Her head throbbed dully, the remnant of a restless night. Yawning, she reached for the phone. Surely it wasn't Alex calling so early. Maybe he'd never call again, he'd been so out of humor when she'd cut short their rendezvous at his cabin. Her behavior had been unforgivable, and she felt a flush of shame. In a vain effort to erase Sam from her mind, she'd responded to Alex's kisses. It hadn't worked, and she'd backed off, pleading an appointment with Dr. Worth. Undoubtedly, Alex's invitation to the cabin had been made with seduction in mind. Now he might give up entirely. To her surprise, she found she didn't really care.

"Meg, honey. How's my favorite client?" It was Jerry Greene, her agent in Los Angeles.

Meg sat up in bed and shivered, pulling the blanket around her against the cool morning air. Jerry wanted a favor or she wouldn't have been promoted to favorite client. "I hope you have good news, Jerry. I could use some."

"How soon can you get a plane to L.A.?"

"To L.A.?" Meg repeated, frowning. Jerry had read her contract, he must know the schedule of the festival. "I can't leave here, Jerry. Opening night is next week."

"Honey, I know you. You're so conscientious you've got your parts down pat. Now listen, this will only take a couple of days. I've got a shampoo commercial for you. It's a lot of money, and if it clicks the residuals could set you up for life."

Although she knew his penchant for exaggeration, Meg still gasped when he named the figure. "For one commercial, Jerry? What do I have to do?"

"Just wash your hair," he laughed. "Can you be here tomorrow? I'll call George Harmon, the director." He paused. "He's the best, you know."

"So I've heard," she replied. "I've never worked with him." Looking across the bedroom into the mirror, Meg pushed back her long dark hair and sighed with resignation, remembering her bank balance. Over the years she'd gradually come to detest modeling—the mindless hours of being moved around like a mannequin, the endless smiles and the demeaning feeling of becoming an object. Over and over again she'd promised herself she'd turn down the offers, but when the acting jobs were too far between or too poorly paying, she'd always had to give in.

"I just can't do it, Jerry. We're rehearsing every minute. I don't see how I can justify my absence, even for two days."

"You can arrange it," Jerry said confidently. "After all, you're only being paid union scale for the festival. They should realize you have to think of the future, too."

"Jerry, I don't know. . . ."

"Go talk to the guy in charge," Jerry interrupted. "I'll bet he'll say it's okay. And don't forget that amount of dough I mentioned."

It was irresistible, the thought of earning enough in one taping to pay her modest bills for several months. It would make things easier for her this fall when she returned to Los Angeles and started looking for work. "All right," she said, letting herself be convinced. "I'll talk to him, check the plane schedule and call you back."

DR. WORTH was understanding. "I realize you have to think of the future, Meg. I know how well prepared you are, and I know you always give your utmost. Two days won't change the world. I think you should go."

Payton came into Dr. Worth's office while they were talking, and he quickly agreed to her absence from *Measure for Measure* rehearsals for two days. "I'll look forward to seeing you on television," he said with a grin.

Catching a glimpse of Carol waiting in the courtyard, Meg guessed Payton had been convinced before he entered the office. The effervescent Carol had hugged Meg joyously when told of Jerry's phone call. As they walked to the theater together, she had plied Meg with questions about filming TV commercials.

"You'd better let Sam know." Dr. Worth's voice had a tentative quality. Meg was aware he'd been afraid there might be problems arising between her and Sam. If there were, it wouldn't be her fault. She was determined to finish the summer with an invisible wall between the two of them. The security provided by the money from this commercial would ease some of her worries. Maybe it would even make it easier to deal with Sam, who seemed to grow more difficult by the day.

Sam was already in the theater preparing for the morning's rehearsal, consulting with the set decorator. After one cool glance at Meg, he ignored her. She decided it would be better to tell him after rehearsal. When he saw how well prepared she was, he couldn't object too strenuously.

Rehearsal went well. At one point, Sam even gave her a grin and said, "Terrific, Meg." For the first time the cast really seemed to blend, everyone working with real empathy to create the world of *Othello*. Theater work was a joy to Meg when this kind of rapport existed in a troupe. In spite of, or maybe because of his toughness, Sam had a talent for bringing a company together.

Waiting to speak to Sam afterward, Meg watched him talking with Joan. Finally, annoyed with Joan's smiling persistence and annoyed with herself for feeling a twinge of jealousy, Meg interrupted. "I'd like to speak to you alone, Sam."

Giving Sam a smile Meg could only interpret as intimate, Joan left them. When she caught herself glaring at Joan's departing back, Meg reminded herself she no longer had proprietary rights to Sam—not even the right to glare at women who made passes at him.

"What's the problem?" Sam asked with a frown. "Does Alexander the Great require your company on my time?"

Gossip was rampant in any theatrical company. No doubt everyone, including Sam, knew she had been at Alex's cabin yesterday.

Quickly she explained to Sam about her opportunity to do a commercial and the plan she had discussed with Dr. Worth.

"Good Lord!" His voice was angry. "It's one week until opening night and you want to miss two rehearsals? Do you think this is a high-school drama club?"

Meg sighed. The old Sam, the one she had loved and married, never flared into anger this way. Why was he so volatile now? She knew he resented her involvement with Alex, but why should he when he was involved with Joan? Suddenly she wished she had taken the plane out that first day when Dr. Worth told her Sam was here. She couldn't have guessed then that she would still be drawn to him, and that he'd still want her.

"You saw me up there today," she said, struggling to keep her voice calm. "You even said I was terrific. I'm a professional actress, Sam. I don't forget a part in two days."

"But you lose your pacing," he protested. Turning away, he slapped his forehead in an overly dramatic gesture. "This company was really rolling today. It was beautiful. If you're gone, we'll lose that."

If only his objections weren't valid. She knew he was right, that he had every reason to be angry with her for going away. But she had gone too far now to turn back. "I promise we won't, Sam." She could barely control her frustration. "You have to understand, I do need the money from this commercial."

"Ah, yes...money," he said coldly. "Always money, fair Meg. Well, go make your money. Apparently that's your number-one priority."

AMID THE MADHOUSE of Los Angeles International Airport, Meg paused to call her friend, Lisa. She was Jerry Greene's receptionist and a would-be actress. When Meg had signed to go to Forest Grove, Lisa had been moving out of her house, sold as part of her divorce settlement. Meg offered the use of her apartment for the summer until Lisa could get settled elsewhere. Today she'd planned to rent a car, leave her bag at the apartment and arrive for the appointment at the studio nearly on time.

A male voice answered the phone. Meg frowned as the voice agreed to call Lisa from the shower.

"Hi, Meg. What are you doing in town?"

"Taping a commercial. Didn't Jerry tell you? Listen, I need a place to bunk for the night. You can put me up, can't you?"

There was a long pause. "It's like this, Meg.... Do you remember Eric?"

Ah yes, Eric...the chronically unemployed actor Lisa had been involved with. So that was his voice.

"He's...well, he's living here with me, and...."

"It would be awkward in a studio apartment," Meg said, barely concealing her disappointment. "Forget it, Lisa." Telling herself she mustn't be upset because Lisa couldn't find a place for her in her own apartment, Meg added, "I'll be back in L.A. the first of September." She hoped Lisa would catch her meaning.

"Sure. I'll take care of everything by then." Lisa did sound a bit chastened. She knew Meg considered Eric a freeloader.

"See you then," Meg said shortly, and hung up.

So far everything had gone wrong, she thought as she made her way to the car-rental desk. Sam had been uncooperative, Lisa had let her down, Jerry hadn't sent a car to meet her, and she would be late for the taping. Not a propitious beginning.

A half hour later, Meg drove the rented car to George Harmon's studio on Melrose Avenue. There she was greeted by his cry of "You're late!"

"My plane was late," she lied, thinking he wouldn't be interested in all her other problems.

George stood in front of her, his bulbous blue eyes inspecting her meticulously. "I was right!" he cried to the crew working in the cavernous studio. "She's perfect." He was short, slightly overweight, with unnaturally brown hair that she realized was a toupee. Appearances aside, she'd seen some of his work, and he was good.

Taking her arm, he drew her toward the small dressing room, at the same time summoning a long-haired young man who had been lounging in a nearby chair. "This is our makeup man," he explained as he seated her in the beautician's chair under the bright lights.

Taking her hair in his hands, he looked at it critically. "You have gorgeous hair." Pursing his lips, he reached out to cup her face in one hand. "Good skin...perfect features." His fingers moved subtly down her neck, and in what he tried to make look like an accident, stroked her breast.

Meg groaned inwardly. So George was one of those. Well, he wasn't the first lecher she'd met in the modeling business. She'd just try to keep out of his reach for the rest of the day. He gave her knee a lingering pat before he left to adjust the cameras.

The wardrobe girl brought a peach satin lace-trimmed robe George had chosen. When Meg appeared in it, George fussed with adjusting it, using the opportunity to caress her bosom several times. The man enraged her. No one had a right to treat her like this...like a thing to be mauled under the pretense of arranging her costume. But she smiled brilliantly as she stepped in front of the cameras, the fan blowing her dark hair as she stood on a false balcony before false palm trees, with a handsome male model staring adoringly at her.

"Beautiful...beautiful..." George kept saying as the cameras ground on and on. The lights were changed and the robe adjusted several more infuriating times.

"Lunch break," George called finally. With a suggestive smile he approached Meg and asked if she would join him for lunch in his office.

"Is that where you keep your casting couch?" she asked in a cold voice.

He managed to change his leer to a look of hurt innocence. "That kind of thing is passé, my dear." But she knew he was furious as he stomped off the set. She was left to have lunch from a caterer's cart with the rest of the crew.

George returned, looking cheerful. Eyeing Meg, he

said, "Okay, honey. We've got the dry hair, now we'll do the shower scene."

"I wasn't aware there was to be a shower scene." Meg wondered whether George had just decided on this to get even with her for not sharing a lunchtime sexual interlude with him.

While the crew rushed to arrange the set, he explained to Meg what he wanted. "You're in the shower. You're using this shampoo you know is going to change your life. I want lots of joy . . . anticipation . . . all that stuff. Understand?"

"Sure," Meg replied. "I use the shampoo, step out onto the balcony and a gorgeous man appears from nowhere . . . no doubt drawn by the scent of the shampoo and my glorious hair."

"Right!" George agreed. "Go ahead and strip now."

"But I don't do nudes, George." She looked at him in astonishment. "Jerry should have told you."

"Meg!" he protested fatuously. "We'll just be photographing the shoulders. How could you not be nude in a shower?" He laughed suggestively and added, "Lots of models would be delighted to do this scene nude just to work with me."

"I have a strapless body suit in my case," Meg said icily. "Let's try it with that."

George hunched his shoulders and spread his hands expressively. "Anything you say." He patted her behind as she turned to go into the dressing room to change.

The afternoon was a nightmare Meg thought would never end. The water in the improvised

shower was cold. George's hands were all over her,
tugging the body suit lower on her breasts, even un-
necessarily straightening the legs by running his
fingers around her thighs. His crew was obviously
used to this for they completely ignored George's
antics. By the time he finally called it a wrap, Meg
was so angry she could have killed him in good conscience. Why did this man think he had the right to
touch her in such an intimate way...to treat her as
an object for his titillation? She detested him with a
violence that shocked her.

Her feelings were so virulent, she was speechless
when he asked her to join him for dinner. Finally
the lie came to her lips.

"I have a date...sorry."

"Can't break it?" he asked with raised eyebrows.

"No...sorry."

He stared at her for a moment in surprise, then
shrugged and nudged his assistant. "Can't win 'em all."

BACK IN HER HOTEL ROOM, Meg flung herself down on
the bed. Tears of frustration stood in her eyes. She
had hated the entire day, everything about it from
the lecherous George to the long hours of posing, her
feet and back aching, her face frozen from smiling,
shivering in the cold shower. Even if George wasn't
a typical director, she'd let the lure of money make
her forget how distasteful it could all be. Never
again, she vowed vehemently. Never again would
she take a modeling assignment. Being treated with
such a lack of respect wasn't worth any amount of
money.

Outside, darkness had fallen. The roar of planes from the airport nearby was muffled, but the air conditioning failed to remove the scent of smog. Meg lay in the dark hotel room, staring at the window. What had possessed her to think this would be a lark? She had been in modeling long enough to know better. Why had she thought she could just fly to Los Angeles, pose for a nice considerate photographer, then share a pleasant dinner with Lisa? Nothing had worked out as she'd planned. Well, she comforted herself, it was over now and she'd be flying back to Forest Grove in the morning. Back to Sam. Suddenly, the hotel room, furnished with the sameness of hotel rooms everywhere, reminded her of another room in Connecticut.

They'd signed that summer with Harold Devore to do the Stratford Shakespearean Festival. It was their first night in town—meeting the cast and crew, drinking champagne at the welcoming party, absorbing the infectious excitement that infused the whole festival. Meg had felt she was floating when she and Sam returned to their hotel.

"It's only the beginning, love," Sam had said, taking her in his arms. "We're going a long way together."

"How far are you willing to go right now?" Meg murmured, nuzzling his earlobe.

Laughing, Sam swept her up in his arms and laid her on the bed. "All the way, baby. Don't trifle with me."

"I'm flown with champagne," she said, looking up into his blue eyes, darkening now with desire. "Undress me, Sam."

Smoothing back her hair, Sam bent to kiss her eyelids, then brushed his mouth against her lips. His fingers caressed her neck, slipping the buttons of her blouse and pushing it off her shoulders along with the straps of her bra. Gently he pulled the garments away, then bent to kiss the pulse at the base of her throat.

Meg lay with eyes closed, luxuriating in the sensations his touch aroused. The warm moistness of his tongue brought her nipples achingly erect. As he stroked her skirt and slip away, she moaned softly, the touch of his hands kindling a flame of desire deep inside her. Tantalizing kisses followed the downward progress of her wispy panty hose as Sam rolled them off. He nibbled at her navel, her hipbones, her thighs, spreading an incredible warmth clear down to the last kiss planted on her toes.

"Sam," she murmured languorously, her body throbbing with longing as he gathered her close in his arms.

His mouth claimed hers in a kiss that left her shaken to her depths. Letting out his breath in a long tremulous sigh, Sam stood up and began to remove his clothes.

"Darling," Meg said, looking up at him lovingly. "Let me...." Sitting up on the side of the bed, she began to unbutton his shirt, her fingers drawing erotic circles in the soft hair on his chest. Watching her with a smoldering look, Sam reached out to gently run his fingers up her bare arms. His loving touch was like a flame on her sensitive skin. Quickly she pushed off his clothing, caressing him as she did. With a groan, Sam pushed her back onto the bed.

Drawing her into his embrace, he kissed her deeply. Responding with all her being, Meg was intoxicated by the taste of him in her mouth. Their bodies strained against each other as though they could never be close enough.

With a soft laugh, Meg pushed him over on his back. "Let me..." she whispered again. She straddled his hips, looking down into eyes hot with desire.

"My love..." he said, reaching to cup his hands around her breasts. "Meg..." he groaned as she eased him inside her and began to move in a slow erotic cadence. Waves of ecstasy engulfed her as Sam's hips moved in rhythm with hers, their bodies joined in a sensuous dance of passion.

Meg quickened her pace, and he responded with wild urgency, their frenzy rising until it burst into blind and incredible rapture. Groaning, Sam thrust deep into her as she cried out her joy. Then he drew her down into his arms, repeating the words over and over..."My love...my love...."

AWAKENING, MEG FOUND her cheeks wet with tears. She had fallen asleep reliving that night with Sam... only one magical night of many in those first two years. It had all been so wonderful. How could it have gone so wrong?

Wiping her eyes, she thought that her marriage had been like this miserable day, begun with such plans and hopes, all gone somehow awry. She had placed the entire blame for the collapse of their relationship on Sam. Now she wondered if there was another side. Had she in some way failed him? His behavior at Forest Grove was both puzzling and infuriating. First he made love to her, then quarreled with her. She couldn't believe he was jealous, or that he wanted any kind of relationship other than sex. Yet how many times had he said, "Can't we start over?" She knew that they could start over, but it would all come out the same unless he had changed. . .or she changed.

You're only fooling yourself. She let the bitter thought rise. *It's ended, whether he accepts it or not.* Yet somewhere in the back of her mind she knew she had not accepted the fact any more than Sam.

Meg stared into the darkness for hours, trying to solve the puzzle, until her tired body surrendered to sleep.

8

IT WAS TWILIGHT when Meg drove the rental car into the parking lot behind the apartment complex. Leaning wearily back in the seat, she sighed. The drive from Las Vegas had been tense and wearing and totally unplanned. Like everything else about this venture, her return to Forest Grove had met with disaster. Los Angeles International had been jammed with the first wave of vacation-bound flights, and her plane delayed just long enough to make her miss the connection for Forest Grove. With only one north-bound plane each day stopping at the little college town, she was stuck in Las Vegas until the flight left at twelve forty-five the next day.

She'd promised Sam and Dr. Worth she'd miss only two rehearsals. Probably she should never have gone to Los Angeles at all, even if she did need the money. It had been selfish of her, and right now she didn't blame Sam for being angry. Imagining how upset he'd be when she didn't show up at the appointed time, Meg consulted the clerk at the car-rental desk.

Yes, it was a four-hour drive to Forest Grove, and yes, they had a car available. Within half an hour Meg was on the northbound desert highway, still seething with frustration.

Now she stretched, stepped out of the car and retrieved her bag from the trunk. A good night's sleep would ease the tension, and she'd be ready for rehearsal bright and early tomorrow.

As she paused to fumble in her purse for the key to her apartment, Meg spotted the note taped to the door. At once she recognized Carol's flamboyant handwriting.

Meg...Schedule changed. Dress rehearsal for *Othello* tonight at seven.

Carol

It was seven-thirty already. Fuming, Meg wondered whether Sam had deliberately had the schedule changed. It wasn't like him to be vindictive, but then he'd been a different Sam this summer. Longing to change from her rumpled blue-linen summer suit, Meg decided there wasn't time. Quickly, she washed her face, combed her hair and hurried across campus.

Sam was prompt as always. When Meg entered the theater courtyard, rehearsal was in progress. In the front row, Sam sat with his note pad on his knee, frowning as he concentrated on the action onstage. *Damn him*, Meg muttered to herself, as she took in the lean figure dressed in blue jeans and a red-and-white rugby shirt, his rugged face intent on the scene being enacted. If only the sight of him didn't stir her as it always did.

Besides Sam, the audience consisted of the assistant director, set decorator, lighting director and costume designer. To Meg's surprise, Alex Martin was seated with Dr. Worth in the second row.

Quietly taking a seat at the end of the row, Meg turned her attention to the stage. The third scene of act 1 had Zach as Othello, explaining how he had won Desdemona's love by telling her of his heroic exploits. Meg smiled in approval as she watched. Zach might be supremely vain, but he had turned into a damned good actor. His voice conveyed the passion of Othello's feeling for Desdemona.

Oh God, Meg thought suddenly. *This scene is Desdemona's first entrance and I'm not even made-up or in costume*. She started to rise to speak to Sam, when the actor playing the part of the Duke spoke: "I think this tale would win my daughter too."

As Desdemona entered with Iago and attendants, Meg stifled a gasp. Joan, wearing her Emilia costume, spoke Desdemona's first lines: "My noble father...."

Seething, Meg watched. The scene was a short one, with Desdemona and Othello exiting to leave Iago and Roderigo onstage to do their plotting.

She should have known! Consumed by indignation, Meg was not even hearing the actors. Joan must have wanted the part all along. Undoubtedly she'd been eager to offer her services as Meg's replacement. A part of her mind knew she was being unreasonable, but her wrath spilled over as the curtain descended at the end of act 1.

Sam turned to Dr. Worth and Alex seated behind him. Apparently he hadn't noticed Meg. "Joan's doing a beautiful job, isn't she?" he asked.

Trembling with anger, Meg stood up and moved toward him. When Alex saw her, he rose quickly and stretched out his hand toward her. In a flash, Meg thought how elegant he looked, dressed in an expensive cream-colored polo shirt and natural-linen slacks. He took her hand and held it tightly. "We have our real Desdemona back with us now."

Sam turned in his seat and scowled at her. "So you've decided to honor us with your presence."

Infuriated by his sarcasm, Meg snapped back. "You had no right to replace me with Joan at the first opportunity."

With a hostile look, Sam asked caustically, "What was I supposed to do, dress up and play the part myself?"

"I told you I'd be back," Meg spoke with asperity. In the back of her mind she knew she was behaving like the proverbial temperamental actress. It was unprofessional and unforgivable, and she didn't care.

"My plane was late. I missed the connecting flight, and I've driven all the way from Las Vegas just to be here in time for rehearsal tomorrow." Her voice rose. "You couldn't wait to replace me, could you? You even changed the rehearsal date. . . ." Suddenly she was aware that the cast and crew onstage were staring. She jerked her hand away from Alex and faced Sam who had risen to frown down at her.

"The dress rehearsal was changed because Payton is ill," he said through clenched teeth. "You're behaving like a paranoid, for God's sake."

Dr. Worth looked dismayed. Waving a hand at the crew, he called, "Take five, everybody. Change the set for act 2."

Taking Meg's arm, he beckoned to Sam. "Let's just step out into the courtyard." His voice was placating. Meg knew that all his worst fears had been realized.

All summer he'd no doubt lived in dread of a blow-up between her and Sam. Here it was.

Alex took a step to follow them, then apparently changed his mind. He remained standing in the theater, glaring at Sam.

In the courtyard, Sam and Meg stood opposite each other like two boxers ready to do battle. Dr. Worth was in the middle as reluctant referee.

"What did you expect me to do while you were off chasing fame and fortune in Hollywood?" Sam's voice was low and furious.

"Now, Sam." Dr. Worth lifted a conciliating hand. "Let's behave like professionals, please. Meg signed for the part of Desdemona. As long as she's able to play it, it's hers. I gave permission for her to be gone two days, and she did call the office from Las Vegas."

"I kept my promise to be back . . . in spite of everything." All the frustrations of the past two days descended on her and her voice trembled.

"I realize that, Meg," Dr. Worth continued soothingly. "*Measure for Measure* was scheduled for dress rehearsal tomorrow, but Payton has what we hope is the twenty-four flu. None of this was done deliberately. You certainly must understand that Sam had to have someone in the role of Desdemona. Joan has played the part before and could step in temporarily."

Sam stood in silence, staring at her in an unreadable way. He'd always hated temperamental actresses who created scenes as she'd just done. Dr. Worth continued talking, obviously practiced at reconciling artistic temperaments. Meg barely heard him explain how she should get into her act 2 costume and the rehearsal would continue.

Defiantly, she stared back at Sam. As his intense blue gaze met hers, the anger melted away. Nothing remained but the inexplicable yearning to be held in his arms and weep away all this dissatisfaction with herself and her life.

The assistant director approached them diffidently. "The set's ready for act 2, Sam. What next?"

Sam's mouth tightened. He gave Meg one last hard look as he turned to answer the young man. *He's terribly angry with me,* Meg thought miserably. She'd behaved like a fool, and nothing between them would ever be mended. *Oh God...* she caught herself. When had she let the hope creep into her heart that it could possibly be mended?

"Skip the makeup, Meg." Sam's voice was rough. "Just get into your costume." He started to walk back into the theater. "I'll speak to Joan."

Meg's anger flared again as she watched him. *Sure go soothe Joan's ruffled feathers, but don't dare spare a kind word for Meg.*

Yet when she returned in her costume, ready to make her entrance in act 2, Joan smiled at her as they stood together in the wings. "Glad you're back, Meg."

Giving her a frosty look, Meg didn't reply. *I'll bet you are,* she wanted to say, *and don't be so damn nice to me.*

All the usual hideous things that mar dress rehearsals happened. Light cues were missed, props misplaced, lines fluffed. Sam's face grew more and more grim as the night wore on. His note pad was filled with comments the cast and crew would hear in detail tomorrow.

It was after midnight when Othello smothered Desdemona in her bed. Lying on the bed onstage, playing the corpse of the murdered wife, listening to the powerful and dramatic final scene, Meg found herself drifting with exhaustion. Unbelievably, she could almost go to sleep onstage. At last Othello stabbed himself in remorse, and fell across the bed beside his dead love. The final words were spoken and the curtain drawn.

SAM SAT in eloquent silence, staring at his notes as the crew cleared the set, changed out of costumes, and prepared to leave the theater. It had been a disastrous rehearsal and no one would dare brave the director's wrath at the moment.

Ever cheerful, Joan returned from changing and announced, "We all know it's traditional that a bad dress rehearsal means a hit on opening night."

Sam allowed himself a tight smile. "Bad dress. Good show," he quoted, shaking his head despairingly. "Brushup tomorrow at nine," he called. "Right here." The cast groaned. He knew they'd hoped for a day off after dress rehearsal. Well, if they'd kept rolling the way they did Monday night, he thought, looking up as Meg came down the steps beside the stage. If Meg had been here . . . . He knew her absence had thrown everyone off, destroyed the timing and rapport the cast had felt that day.

Watching her as she crossed toward Alex, who

held out his hands toward her, Sam felt as though someone had punched him in the solar plexus. Damn it, he had to stop wanting her. A primitive urge to punch Alex in his smiling mouth shook Sam. There was a sharp sound and he realized he'd snapped his pencil in two.

Meg...Meg. His eyes followed her. She turned to look at him as though she'd heard him call her name, an expectant expression on her face.

"You've done it better, Meg. Let's hope you will again." Once said, the words seemed ill chosen and harsh. He'd meant to be encouraging, but it hadn't come out that way. The flash of anger in her eyes told him she'd misinterpreted them. Meg was a good actress and one bad rehearsal wouldn't crush her, but he should have said something different, or nothing at all.

He caught her hostile look as Joan sat down beside him. Why was Meg so antagonistic toward Joan? There was no understudy program at the festival and Joan had seemed a lifesaver when he needed a Desdemona. Meg should have understood that. She had acted unreasonable and spoiled. He loved her so much he'd have done anything rather than hurt her. Why didn't she know that? Maybe the damned rich playboy had something to do with the change in her.

Without another word, Meg walked out of the theater with Alex beside her. Sam's eyes followed them, a sick sensation filling his chest. He scarcely heard Joan's continuing chatter.

SEATED IN THE SOFT COMFORT of the Mercedes, Meg closed her eyes wearily.

"A rough night," Alex said sympathetically. "I'll bet you haven't had dinner either. I'll have Kim fix a snack and then I'll take you home."

Meg nodded agreement, glad to have someone thinking of her comfort and taking care of her for a change.

Seated on the terrace, with the pool gleaming beyond and soft music playing on the stereo, Meg and Alex ate the omelet Kim had quickly prepared. The wine he served was dry and crisp. Its warmth spread quickly along her tense muscles. For the first time in three days, she relaxed.

"The whole thing was unforgivable," Alex was saying. "You don't need that kind of hassle, Meg." His eyes were warm with admiration as he watched her through the veil of his cigarette smoke. "A beautiful woman like you should be protected and cared for, not badgered by a martinet like Sam Richardson."

"He's the director," Meg said vaguely, thinking she had been too tired and too hungry to drink the wine.

"No reason to treat you like that," Alex said in a resentful tone. "I can't help thinking he's being vindictive toward you, just because you're his ex-wife."

"Maybe," Meg murmured. "But Sam's not really like that. Anyway, let's not talk about Sam. I've had enough of that for one night."

"Why do you do it, Meg?" Alex gave her an inquiring look. "Are you really happy with this kind of life?"

Meg shrugged, drifting pleasantly on the effects of the wine.

Leaning back in his chair, Alex smiled reflectively. "Think about this: my philosophy of life is to do only what pleases me and makes me happy. I don't want goals, and at this point I have no need to struggle to achieve anything. Most of all, I don't want storms in my life . . . only untroubled waters."

"Sounds hedonistic, but wonderful," Meg replied with a wry smile. She didn't add that it occurred to her how easy it would be to develop such a philosophy when there was unlimited money in the bank. But, she wondered, could even money help one avoid all of life's storms?

Kim cleared away the dishes and disappeared into the house. Alex crushed out his cigarette, rose and stood before Meg, holding out his hands. Standing up, Meg went into his arms. His mouth took hers in a kiss that was at once tender and passionate. She could almost feel his desire for her growing as his arms tightened around her and his lips grew more demanding.

Drawing away, he whispered, "You're the most exquisite woman I've ever known." He smiled tenderly at her. "I could give you a world worthy of that beauty, Meg. The whole world. . . ."

Her battered ego soothed by his words, Meg leaned into his embrace, returning his kiss. But much as she willed it, no fire kindled.

Slowly she extricated herself from the growing urgency of his kisses. "I'm desperately tired, Alex."

"Of course you are." His voice was contrite. "Forgive me." His mouth touched hers softly. "We'll continue this conversation tomorrow."

9

APPLAUSE WASHED over her in warm approving waves. Basking in the sounds of approbation, Meg knew this was the true reward of the theater. The cast of *Othello* took their bows after the opening night performance. First, the entire cast, then the supporting players, then the four leads: Othello, Desdemona, Iago and Emilia. The volume of sound increased. People began to stand and applaud. Several "Bravos!" echoed through the small theater. Then Meg and Zach were alone on stage, the entire audience standing, applauding madly. "Bravo! Bravo!"

Zach stepped back and held his hand out toward Meg, presenting her for the audience's approval. After a deep curtsy, she returned the courtesy to Zach. Again the volume of applause increased. Zach bowed and turned to take Meg's hand. Together they bowed again, then ran from the stage. The applause continued.

In the crush backstage, the stage director was urging the supporting cast back for another bow. Grinning, Zach grabbed Meg's hand and led her back onstage. Once more the other actors took their bows, then Meg and Zach were alone, smiling at each other as the sound rolled across the footlights.

A young man from the festival office was standing near the apron of the stage holding a sheaf of flowers up to Meg. As she reached down to take them, he gallantly kissed her hand. The audience roared their approval. Once more... the shouts of "Bravo!" and the increased tempo of clapping hands. Then the two of them hurried offstage.

Sam was pushing through the excited crowd backstage, waving directions at the players. "Take another bow... they loved you! Enjoy it!"

Breathless, Meg stood again onstage before the reverberating theater, bowing, smiling with Zach. The young man with flowers reappeared, carrying a huge bouquet of red roses. *Alex!* Meg thought as she bent to receive them. How sweet of him and how typical. At once she spotted him standing in the second row, applauding madly. Impulsively she blew him a kiss as she stood with the armful of red roses making a brilliant contrast to the white clinging nightdress of the death scene.

Zach squeezed her hand and nodded toward the stage apron where the young man still waited. Meg stepped forward again and he handed her a nosegay of violets.

The whole scene seemed to shatter. Trembling, Meg stepped back, holding the nosegay against her breast. Sam! So many other opening nights those violets had conveyed his love and approval. There had been violets for Juliet at Central Park, violets at Stratford, even in seedy off-Broadway playhouses. Did Sam realize what those violets meant to her? Yearning filled her and tears burned her eyes. She felt

Zach's hand tighten on her arm, and realized she had lost her stage presence as she was caught up in an aching flood of memory.

Again they went through the routine of carefully choreographed bows, smiles and gestures. The audience seemed reluctant to let them go. They ran off-stage only to be recalled for a final bow. The stage lights darkened and the houselights came up. Applause died away as the crowd began to move out of the theater.

Backstage was a madhouse, with cast and crew milling around, everyone talking at once. A grinning Sam submitted to hugs and kisses from the entire female cast. Dr. Worth was plowing his way through the crush, shouting for attention.

"I didn't want to cause anyone stress by mentioning this before the performance," he said as the noise died to a buzz. "We had two top-notch critics in our audience tonight. One from New York and the other from the *Los Angeles Times*. From what they said to me, the reviews are going to be terrific."

Joyful shouts greeted his statement.

Zach threw his arms around Meg exuberantly. "You were marvelous, Meg."

Returning his hug, she looked at him and said sincerely, "You're one of the finest Othello's I've seen, Zach. If those critics agree with me, you've got it made."

Zach's grin faded as he shot a hostile glance across the room at Sam. "In spite of Sam Richardson."

Before she could reply they were interrupted. Payton was shaking Zach's hand, congratulating him.

Carol had flung her arms around Meg, saying incoherent things praising Meg's performance. In the excitement of the moment, Zach's unreasonable hostility toward Sam faded from her mind.

Grinning widely, accepting accolades, handshakes and hugs, Sam slowly made his way across the backstage area to confront his stars.

"Zach," he said, holding out his hand. "That was a masterful job. If the critics aren't impressed by your Othello, they should be watching situation comedies on TV."

"Thanks, Sam." Zach's voice was noncommittal. "I never doubted I could do it." Sam seemed to miss the underlying meaning of the words for he had turned to look fondly down at Meg.

"Incredible," he said, taking her hand and kissing it. "There wasn't a man in the audience who wouldn't have murdered for love of your Desdemona tonight." Slowly he released her hand. "Even me," he added in a low emotional voice.

The old sensation of drowning in his deep blue gaze overwhelmed Meg. Her throat clogged so that it was a moment before she could speak. "Thanks for the violets, Sam," she murmured, wanting everything to be as it once was, wanting to be in his arms. He had exchanged elated casual hugs and kisses with all the other women in the cast, and only kissed her hand.

"An old tradition," he replied, looking deep into her eyes, unsmiling.

"Sam . . . you're the world's greatest director!" Joan burst upon them, throwing her arms around Sam and giving him a gleeful kiss. Turning to Meg, she added, "You were simply great, Meg." Sam's arm remained casually around Joan's shoulders.

Fighting the pain rising from the core of her at this evidence of intimacy, Meg managed to thank Joan and congratulate her on her performance. Looking up, she saw Alex enter the backstage area, his eyes searching the crowd. At once he began to make his way toward her.

The night's triumph dimmed by her burst of envy toward Joan and by the painful memories awakened by Sam's violets, Meg turned eagerly to Alex.

"You were superb," he said, smiling, bending to kiss her cheek and murmuring in her ear, "Shall we get out of here?"

"I'll change and meet you outside," Meg replied. She ignored Sam's quizzical look. As she pushed her way toward the stairs leading to the tunnel and the dressing rooms, she glanced back. Sam stood talking to Alex, his arm still around Joan's shoulders.

"Tired?" Alex asked as the Mercedes pulled out of the theater parking lot.

Leaning back against the soft leather seats, Meg sighed. "Exhausted. But keyed up, of course." To herself, she was unwilling to admit that some of the joy had gone from the night's success because she could not share it with Sam. But there was Alex, she chided herself. Alex, who sent red roses and was always there with everything prearranged for her, calm, gentle, considerate, comfortable.

"Kim has a late snack waiting for us," Alex told

her. "And a bottle of Taittinger on ice." He gave her a fond smile. "Nothing short of champagne is adequate for the performance you gave tonight.

"You're sweet, Alex. This company seems to work together extraordinarily well." She gave a short disclaiming laugh. "Not that we're all so crazy about each other. Maybe it's just that our talents seem complementary." *Or maybe*, she thought, *it's Sam Richardson's strong and competent hand at the helm. Oh damn! Stop thinking of Sam. Enjoy this man who offers comfort and praise along with caviar and champagne.*

With impulsive gratitude, Meg reached over and covered his hand with hers. "Dear Alex. You're just the man to bring one down from the top of a roller coaster."

In the light from the dashboard, she saw that he was not pleased. "I'm not sure that's a compliment. Maybe I'd rather be the one to take you up the roller coaster."

Meg laughed quickly, realizing her impetuous words had irked him. "I'm looking for the right words, Alex, and not doing very well." Squeezing his hand, she added, "I've got it! You're my safe harbor—and I love it."

He stopped the car before the lighted ranch house and turned toward her. Drawing her into his arms, Alex's mouth claimed hers in a demanding kiss. He wanted to be more than a safe harbor, Meg knew. She must have always known he wouldn't be satisfied with that kind of relationship. Because she felt very alone tonight, she kissed him in return. But she felt herself withdraw as his hand came down to cup her breast, and his tongue teased at her lips. Gently, she pushed him away.

"I'm ready for that champagne, Alex," she said with a forced laugh.

WEARILY, MEG CLOSED the apartment door and drew a deep ragged breath. In her mind she tried to recapture the thrill of that triumphant moment onstage tonight, with applause thundering around her. How wonderful it would be if life could be lived always at such a glorious peak of experience. But, and she dropped her thin evening sweater over the back of a chair...*perhaps if it could we wouldn't appreciate the triumph when it arrived.*

The whole aftermath of the performance had been a letdown. Alex had obviously planned to make love to her tonight, and it had taken all her charm to persuade him she was too exhausted to consider seduction. With a prick of pain she thought of Sam's obvious attachment to Joan. The whole apartment complex was dark, and Meg tried not to think of who was sleeping with whom.

Sighing, she glanced around. Carol had brought her flowers from the theater and placed them in vases: the sheaf of gladiolus from the festival committee, Alex's red roses—and in a coffee mug, the nosegay of violets.

Picking up the violets, Meg held them to her nose. Unlike the eastern variety Sam used to send, these had no scent. Symbolic, it seemed, of her marriage and her life. The violets were beautiful, but without the fragrance there was no magic, they were simply mundane purple flowers. Tears of regret flooded her eyes, and she flung the nosegay across the room.

THE COMEDY OF ERRORS opened the following night. Although the audience response was not as overwhelming as it had been for *Othello*, everyone agreed it had gone well. The laughs came in all the right places. While the pace needed tightening, it was a good performance. When Alex arrived, Meg pleaded exhaustion. She returned to her apartment and slept the clock around.

At his insistence, they shared a late dinner after Wednesday's opening performance of *Measure for Measure*. He was to fly to Denver on business the following morning, and kept saying he wished she could accompany him.

His demands were growing more ardent each time they were together, and Meg was finding it more difficult to refuse without hurting his feelings. Watching his handsome profile as he drove her home in hurt silence, she wondered what was wrong with her. Alex was everything a woman could ask for in a lover—considerate, attentive and attractive. If Sam had never been a part of her life, perhaps it would have been easy to fall in love with Alex Martin. She'd do it anyway, if she had good sense. He offered more in a material way than any man she'd known, and he was a wonderful person in the bargain.

You're a fool, she told herself, and gave Alex such a fervent good-night kiss, he stared at her in surprise.

DOFFING THE RED fright wig, Meg took her time removing the heavy makeup, the warts and the long nose of Mistress Overdone. Smiling at her image in the mirror, she considered how much she was enjoying this part. It was so completely in contrast to Desdemona.

Outside in the theater courtyard, a cast party was getting under way. Meg could hear someone playing show tunes on a piano. As the clink of glasses helped raise the decibels of sound filtering down into the dressing room, she hurried to change. Slipping into her dress—a soft cotton in subtle shades of pink with a wide square neckline, short puffed sleeves and a full skirt—Meg felt a sense of anticipation. Was it because she wouldn't have to be concerned about Alex's reaction and could simply relax and enjoy herself tonight?

Walter McGrath was at the piano surrounded by a bevy of admiring young women. Zach was holding court for his female admirers near the improvised bar where Dr. Worth was acting as bartender. Payton seemed to have taken charge of the proceedings for he was directing placement of lights on the outdoor greenshow stage. Tables had been set up on one side of the courtyard where Carol and Joan were arranging snacks from the local deli.

Taking a deep breath, Meg headed toward the bar. Zach moved away from his fans long enough to get a glass of wine for her. "Did you see the review from the *L.A. Times*?" he asked, trying to act nonchalant.

Meg laughed. "I think Dr. Worth must have made two thousand copies of it." Sobering, she added, "If the New York reviews are that good, you'll be swamped with offers."

He grinned complacently. "You too, Meg. With all that talent in one cast how could we miss?"

"Maybe the director had something to do with it," Meg said wryly, knowing Zach wouldn't like the idea.

"Like hell!" he burst out. "We'd have been that good without a director. Sam Richardson's reputation is based on luck."

"That's not true, Zach." Meg's voice was indignant. Zach's grudge against Sam was showing.

"He turned me down for the lead in *The Stamp Collector*, you know—" Zach's eyes narrowed, his handsome mouth twisted bitterly "—even though the producer wanted me. That part was a career maker." He cast a look of distaste at Sam across the courtyard. "I was that close to real success—the big time, not a regional thing like this."

"This has been good for you, Zach," Meg replied, intending to placate him but unwilling to concede that Sam had damaged his career in any way.

One of the young girls waiting for Zach came up and took his arm, looking suggestively into his face. Zach winked at Meg. "Well, it's a ball, anyway," he grinned, allowing himself to be led away.

"What a metamorphosis." It was Sam standing beside her, smiling. "You look terrific, Meg. When I see *Measure for Measure*, I can't believe it's you up there playing that ugly old broad."

"I assume that's a compliment." Buoyed by his admiration and the exhilarated air of the party, she gave him a teasing look.

"You can bet it is." His eyes held hers, darkening with intensity.

Determined to maintain the lighthearted mood, Meg chided him. "The Shakespearean word is *bawd* not *broad*. Careful of those anachronisms."

Sam laughed easily. Taking a sip of wine, he observed, "I don't remember you ever doing comedy before. . .and you're so good at it."

"The depths of my talent are unplumbed, dear director," she said mockingly. "Actually I had a small part in *Plaza Suite* for six whole weeks at the Mark Taper Forum Theater. It was hard work, but I loved it."

His eyes gleamed as he smiled down at her. "You didn't tell me about that . . . but then you haven't told me much in the past year, have you?"

Sipping her wine, Meg didn't answer. *No deep discussions about our problems tonight*, she wanted to say. *Tonight is for fun.*

"I thought you were doing mostly TV." He chuckled and looked a bit shamefaced. "Do you know I used to want to call you every time I saw your face on television?"

Touched, Meg took a moment to gain control of her voice. "I didn't think you watched TV."

"Didn't used to." There was a world of meaning in the words.

A microphone shrieked. Glad for the interruption, Meg saw that Payton was standing on the stage.

"Ladies and germs!" he said in a jocular tone. The exhilarated crowd laughed at the old chestnut of a joke. "It's a theory of mine that actors never get tired of showing off. We're throwing the evening open for an impromptu talent show. If you dramatic actors want to do a dance . . . or whatever . . . all you have to do is volunteer."

"What are you going to do, Payton?" someone yelled, just as Carol came to stand beside Meg and Sam. She held a plate of ham rolls and potato salad.

"It just so happens," Payton said, making his voice deep and impressive, "that my middle name is Blackstone. If my assistant will come up here, we will amaze and confound you with some incredible feats of prestidigitation."

"Eat this to keep up your strength," Carol said, rolling her eyes expressively. She handed the plate to Meg and hurried to join Payton onstage. Laughing, Sam shook his head and took one of the ham rolls Meg offered.

Payton's magic tricks were strictly amateur quality and not very deceptive. The mood of the crowd was so exultant, they clapped and shouted hilarious approval even when Carol dropped the Chinese rings and they came apart with no help from Payton.

Walter McGrath bounded onto the stage as Payton and Carol descended. "I'd like to confide to all of you my most secret dream," he said with a grin. "I've always wanted to be an opera singer. Since Payton's given me the chance, I'm damned well going to sing 'Figaro.'" He shook a finger at the crowd. "Woe be unto anyone who dares leave while I'm performing."

Joan had taken her place at the piano and accompanied Walter's credible, if broadly acted, rendition of the clown's lament.

When he finished, he bowed deeply to his cheering

audience, then asked them to insist that Dr. Worth perform. Meg and Sam exchanged amused glances as Dr. Worth almost succeeded in breaking the mood of the party by reciting from *Hamlet*.

The crowd responded with thunderous applause as though to restore the lighthearted mood. Dr. Worth then announced that Sam would perform.

"Watch this, love." Sam grinned at her, and his arm went around her shoulders in a brief embrace.

When he took the stage, Meg felt her heart leap in a disturbingly familiar way. That long lean body, the graceful way he moved . . . an old ache revived inside her, and she could not put it away.

Apparently, he had planned his performance with Joan, now at the piano, for she immediately began playing tunes from the musical *Cabaret*. Meg drew in her breath and closed her eyes, remembering with a pang the night the two of them had gone to see Joel Grey's marvelous performance. *Oh Sam*, she wanted to cry. *We shared so much, and now it's all gone.*

Sam was carrying a top hat and cane from the prop department. Watching him get into position before the mike, grinning in a conspiratorial manner at the crowd, Meg had an insane impulse to run from the courtyard. If only she could flee to someplace where there would be no memory of love.

Sam began to sing. He had always liked to sing, and she used to tease him about being off-key, even though it gave his voice a special charm. Now he sang a medley of tunes from *Cabaret*, waving his top hat and twirling his cane at appropriate intervals. The tempo increased as he swung into the words of "Money, Money."

Damn you...damn you, Meg thought wildly as the words repeated over and over...money makes the world go around...world go around.... His whole performance was directed at her, it seemed—a reminder of their failure. The pain was almost unbearable, but Meg stood amid the crowd, trying with all her strength to control her facial expression, wishing she could just disappear.

Sam bowed to the applause, grinning broadly. Joan jumped up from the piano and ran to the stage, throwing her arms around Sam and kissing him. Laughter and applause resounded through the courtyard. Meg could still hear it when she was halfway across the campus.

10

A SOOTHING FLOW of water from the hot shower drained away some of Meg's misery. *You're not in love with Sam Richardson, director,* she told herself bitterly. *You're still in love with the charming gentle young man you once married, and he no longer exists.* That Sam would never have hurt her in this way. He'd grown vindictive and hateful. Her tears mingled with the hot water as she tried to come to terms with what seemed bitter reality.

As she toweled herself dry, the doorbell rang. If she hadn't left the lights on, she'd just ignore it. Undoubtedly, it was Carol. She must have noticed Meg making her hurried exit from the party and guessed something was wrong. Caring person that she was, Carol would follow and try to comfort. With a sigh, Meg thought that she didn't want comfort right now. What she wanted was to be alone—to lick her wounds, as the old cliché went.

When she opened the front door, she knew her first instinct had been the right one. Sam's tense face stared at her out of the darkness. For an instant, she thought her heart would burst with pain.

"I want to talk to you." His voice held a pleading note.

"If it's business, it can wait until tomorrow," she replied coldly, recovering from the shock of seeing him standing there. "If it's personal, there's nothing more to be said." Realizing she'd failed to chain the door, she tried to push it shut only to see his expression grow more determined.

After a brief struggle, his superior strength won. Closing the door behind him, Sam leaned against it, waiting.

Breathing heavily from her exertions, Meg glared at him. At the same time, she was achingly aware of the sandy hair curling at the open neck of his blue tattersall shirt, the pulse pounding in his throat, the strong line of his chin, his mobile mouth, and at last those blue eyes that seemed to be trying to look into her soul. Trying to hang on to her self-possession, Meg tightened the sash of her terry robe around her waist.

"What do you want?" she demanded.

Unexpectedly, Sam reached out and pulled the pins from her hair as he had so many times in the past. It fell in a dark cloud around her shoulders. His face softened. "God, you're beautiful." His voice was unsteady.

"Leave me alone, Sam," she cried, touched by the gesture and furious at herself for responding to it. She turned away, determined to lock him out of her bedroom.

Sam's hands grasped her shoulders. He looked so contrite that a war of tenderness and anger wrenched her heart.

"Meg, love." His voice was entreating. "When I

saw you run out of the party tonight, I knew it was my fault, that I'd hurt you . . . and I didn't mean to, not ever."

"Sure!" She jerked away from him. "It was just a little personal dig. Money makes the world go around, Sam." Trembling, she faced him. "You think I don't know that very well? Maybe you've forgotten that it was my money that made our world go around when we were married." Her shaking voice rose as she struggled for control. "Sure, I was preoccupied with money. I had to earn most of it . . . and I had to give up a lot of things that were important to me for that reason."

"Meg . . ." Sam laid his hand on her shoulder. With an angry gesture she pushed it off, wanting him to hurt as much as she could.

Without warning, Sam reached out and pulled her into his arms. Struggling to free herself, Meg pushed against his chest, but the strong arms held. At last she realized he was determined to hold her and she couldn't win against his strength. Ignoring the clamor inside her, she stood stiff and cold in his embrace.

"Why must money always come between us?" he asked sadly.

"Not money." She made no attempt to hide the bitterness in her voice. "Just the lack of it. That, and the fact that you'd do anything to get money for what you want to do."

Sam winced as though she'd struck him. "So that's still festering? Damn it, I explained it all to you. Is money the only thing that's important to you? Is that why you're encouraging Alex—because he's rich?"

Because there was a germ of truth in what he said, Meg bristled defensively. "It's none of your business!" She flung the words at him and tried to break out of his embrace.

The blue eyes looking down at her were as vulnerable as a child's. His expression aroused such a bittersweet pain, she felt her eyes sting. She'd forgotten the way his mouth turned down at one corner when he was hurt or unhappy.

"Aren't we even on the same wavelength anymore, Meg?" he asked ruefully. "Do you know why I chose that music for tonight? Because I was remembering when the two of us saw *Cabaret* in New York. It was one of the greatest nights of my life, love. I thought it was for you, too." The blue eyes darkened with regret. "I never guessed that one song would strike you the way it did."

Meg scarcely heard him, her mind filled with the memory of that glorious evening. The show had been superb, and afterward in their cold apartment they drank a bottle of wine, sang songs from the show, laughed and made love.

"Oh, Sam. . . ." Defeated, Meg leaned her forehead against his broad shoulder, trying to stem the tears that threatened to overflow.

His arms tightened comfortingly around her, and his cheek pressed against her hair. With one hand he cupped the back of her head, turning her face to meet his kiss.

Meg's response was instinctive. All resistance, all anger, melted away with the sweetness of his mouth on hers. When he held her like this it was as though the bad times had never been. Their reaction to each other was as new and breathless as the first time. Her hands moved along his shoulders and down his back in a loving caress. Pressing against him, she felt his arousal and her body responded, suddenly aflame with longing.

Gently, Sam's hands moved down over her body. She heard his sharp intake of breath when he realized she was naked beneath the terry robe. Loosening the sash, he slowly pushed the robe off her shoulders, all the while covering her face, her eyes, her throat, with tantalizing kisses.

The robe fell into a heap at her feet. Naked in his arms, Meg reveled in the touch of his hands as they ignited every nerve in her body.

"Sam..." she murmured, leaning dizzily against him, seething with desire. Reaching up, she took his face in her hands. Their lips met in complete surrender.

In one quick movement, Sam lifted her in his arms and carried her the few steps to the bedroom. While he switched off the lights, Meg lay on the comforter watching him with growing anticipation. A pale stream of moonlight poured through the high window, lighting his lean strong body as he quickly undressed. Then he lay beside her, his arms enveloping her in a fierce embrace, his tongue plundering her mouth.

Her body arched against his, already wild with desire. But she knew he would not take her yet. Sam knew her too well...knew every touch and caress that would bring her to the most frenzied heights of pleasure.

Slowly his mouth trailed fiery kisses down her throat. Lips and tongue combined to bring her breasts and nipples to firm mounds of aching desire. Sensation piled on sensation as his hands and his mouth moved from the pulse at the base of her throat down to the pulsating core of her.

The feel of his strong muscled back beneath her fingertips sent pleasurable tremors through her. As the intensity of her desire mounted, Meg let her hands drift down his body, exploring his most intimate sensitive spots. The fierce ache between her thighs intensified until she almost cried out the urgency of her longing.

Moaning with pleasure, Sam came into her. With the blazing magic of their joining, a soft cry broke from Meg's throat.

"My love...my love...." The words were incredibly sweet, whispered breathlessly in Meg's ear. Their mouths met in a deep soul-searing kiss. The rhythm of their bodies quickened, soaring on a wave of ecstasy. They were one body, one being, united completely in that final endless moment of rapture.

SAM STIRRED and slowly came awake to the distant sound of voices echoing across the dark campus. A pale glow of moonlight slanted through the window of Meg's bedroom. Turning, he leaned on his elbow and gazed down into her sleeping face.

Her loose dark hair fanned across the white pillow, framing her pale features like a shadowy halo. With one finger, he gently brushed a strand of hair from her cheek. She sighed in her sleep. The warmth of her body, the sweet feminine scent of her had already aroused him. God, how he loved her. He couldn't look at her without wanting her, couldn't remember a really happy moment in his life since they'd parted.

He'd pinned all his hopes on a reconciliation at Forest Grove. He'd even dreamed of going back to New York together, recreating what had once been between them. Still, every time they came close, Meg flared up with that unreasonable anger of hers. Why was she so unwilling to hear what he needed to tell her? They had been one for three wonderful years, with the same goals, the same aspirations. Then suddenly, she'd opted out. It couldn't have been the scene with Linda. Surely Meg knew he'd never been unfaithful. And the money he'd borrowed from his dad—he could have put the figures on paper to prove his integrity in that deal, but she wouldn't listen.

"Meg." Even her name tasted sweet to him as he whispered it softly. Resisting the urge to gather her up in his arms and kiss her awake, Sam lay still. His eyes devoured her soft sleepy face, love for her filling every cell of his being.

With a wry smile, he thought that there was nothing virtuous in his celibacy. He simply didn't want anyone but Meg. A few weeks of madly playing the field after she'd filed for divorce had proved that. Joan would have been willing to indulge in a cheerful no-strings summer affair with him, even though she'd told him about her long-term relationship with a fellow professor. The man was an archaeologist, presently on a summer dig in Mexico. Sam had known Joan's type before. She was good company and had a great body. To her, sex was just 'fun,' not the deep emotional commitment it had been to Meg and to him. Joan had made her intentions clear at once. When he didn't respond, she settled amiably for friendship. She was intelligent, fun and helpful with his play, but she wasn't Meg.

With a sigh, Meg stirred and opened her eyes. At first she looked startled, then her deep eyes softened. She reached one hand to lay her palm gently against his cheek. Catching her hand in his, Sam kissed each fingertip lingeringly. He watched her eyes soften as the caress aroused her senses.

Sam bent to touch her lips, every part of his body aching with love for her. The warm softness beneath his mouth, the intimate touch of her fingertips on his shoulders, aroused him to fever pitch. Her willing lips opened to his tongue, and their bodies came together with a new hunger.

Breathless, still intoxicated by the way they had soared together to that final climax, Sam lay with Meg held close against him. As his heartbeat slowed, he surrendered to a feeling of delicious weakness, sated with love.

Meg gave a soft satisfied sigh. Her warm breath blew gently against his throat. With an expression of utter contentment, she curled against him.

"Meg," he murmured. "What we have together is so good."

Turning to face him on the pillow, Meg gave him a wistful smile. "Until we get out of bed," she said, sadness in her voice.

"I just keep loving you, sweet Meg. I can't seem to

stop. Sam buried his face against her fragrant throat. "You're the only woman I've ever wanted."

There was a long silence. Sam found his body tensing as he waited, longing to hear her say the words, "I love you."

Meg made a strangled sound. "The only woman?" she asked in a tight voice. "Who was the only woman last night—Joan?"

Sitting up in the bed, Sam stared down into her face, seeing the bitter lines that had suddenly formed around her mouth. Condemnation darkened her eyes. "What brought that on?" he asked coldly.

Meg refused to meet his eyes. "You have been sleeping with her, haven't you? Everyone in the company knows it."

Anger blazed in him. He deserved her trust, he always had, and she continued to withhold it. "Even if I deny it, you know it?" Only with an effort did he manage to keep his voice even.

"It's pretty obvious," was the sharp reply.

"Damn it!" Sam sat up and swung his feet to the floor. There was a deep ache in his chest, a coldness as though something within him were dying.

"You can't ever trust me, can you? I guess that's why we no longer have a marriage."

He pulled on his clothes quickly. From the corner of his eye he could see her watching, her face closed and unreadable. When she didn't speak again, he didn't bother to say good-night.

Circumspect even in anger, Sam closed the apartment door quietly. He felt like slamming it. Almost at once, the night air cooled his wrath. Morosely shoving his hands in his back pockets, he walked slowly back to his apartment.

Despite the divorce papers hidden away, unsigned, Sam had always felt that the bond between them endured. Even with a continent separating them, he'd felt a connection to Meg, eagerly scanning the trade papers for her name, glad for the sense of joy the unexpected sight of her face in a photograph or on TV brought to him.

He'd been so sure he could put the relationship back together here at Forest Grove. Then he'd allowed his jealousy and pain to run away with his better judgment. He'd been harsh with her in ways he never had when they were married. *Self-indulgent, jealous bastard!* he swore at himself.

But there would be no more chances. As soon as the lovemaking was over, Meg was once more unforgiving. Even though she was dead wrong in her judgment, she'd never trust him again. He couldn't live with that, no matter how much he loved her.

The sense of loss was complete. The marriage, and all the love that went with it, was ended. Only tonight could he truly believe it was over.

11

Long after Sam had gone, Meg lay awake, staring at the pale square of window, trying to sort out her emotions. Why did Sam think that making love could erase all the conflicts that had torn them apart? He didn't seem to understand that their marriage hadn't really dissolved the moment she saw him with another woman who was obviously bent on seducing him. It was a long accumulation of disappointments and resentment, unshared and unreconciled.

Yes, she admitted, she could forget them when she was in his arms. In no other place did she feel so complete, so at one with the world. But it was all so fragile when reality intruded. Life could not be lived in bed. One had to have respect and love in every aspect of a relationship. Sex was never enough, no matter how good it was.

At last she slept, to be awakened late in the morning by the distant sound of church bells. In the kitchen, she sleepily made coffee, wondering idly why Carol hadn't appeared as she usually did. It crossed her mind that Carol might have spent the night in Payton's apartment after the party. She hoped so.

A letter from her father, quickly read, lay on the kitchen counter. One glance at it brought a sudden wave of homesickness, and Meg picked up the phone. After all, Sunday rates were on.

"Meg!" Ben Driscoll cried when she said hello. "Sweetheart, I was just thinking about you...and missing you."

"You sound great, dad," she said, then hesitated. "Is mom there?"

"No, she went to the theater again today," he replied, as easily tolerant of his wife's absences as he had always been. "She's so excited about the chance to direct this new play, *Spirit*, she spends every minute she can at the theater. You know how much she's always wanted to direct."

"Sure, that's great." Meg's voice was flat with disappointment. Why would she expect anything else? Her mother had bestowed loving words and hugs in passing for years. A thousand images flashed through her mind of promises made and broken because the theater was more important than Meg's dance recital or award dinner. Quickly dismissing those old resentments, Meg asked, "How are you doing, dad?"

"I guess I told you in my letter that I'm working with the inner-city kids in Chicago this summer," he replied.

"Yes, that always concerns me. I hope it isn't too much for you. Those kids can be tough."

"Honey, I can be tough too. Would you believe I've got them doing Shakespeare?"

"You can do anything," she answered affectionately, wanting to tell him he was the anchor of her life, but knowing they would both end up in tears.

"I just wish we had the time to fly out to see your

Desdemona," he said. "I know you're terrific, but with this teaching assignment of mine and your mother's play, well. . . ."

"I understand." A sense of relief overwhelmed Meg, with the knowledge that her parents wouldn't be coming to Forest Grove. She had never mentioned that Sam was here. Her parents were crazy about Sam and brokenhearted over the divorce. If she told them, they'd start hoping for a reconciliation. That would be unfair to them—and to her.

As though he could read her thoughts across the miles, her father's next words were couched in careful tones. "Have you heard from Sam? I tried to call him last week and he's not in New York."

"We're divorced, dad." At least she wasn't lying to him, just avoiding the truth.

"I know, honey. I . . . well, you know how I feel."

"Sure." Meg struggled for control of her voice, almost sorry now that she had impulsively called him. He and Sam had become such good friends, she knew he'd never stop hoping they'd get back together. Quickly changing the subject, she asked, "How's my old friend, Max?"

"Right here beside me," her father answered with a laugh. "He's got an eager look on his face as though he knows it's you on the phone." He chuckled again. "How are you getting along with Max's look-alike, Dr. Worth?"

"He's a nice man," Meg replied. She was seized by another wave of homesickness. She could picture her father in his untidy study, and Max with his muzzle on dad's knee, gazing hopefully into his face. If she was less unhappy about last night, this would have been a more satisfying conversation. As it was, Meg barely managed to control her emotions through their goodbyes.

After she hung up, Meg wandered aimlessly around the apartment, drinking her coffee. Back in the bedroom, she quickly made up the bed, trying not to think of the ecstatic hours she'd spent there with Sam last night.

As she caught his scent from the pillow, Meg closed her eyes tightly, shaken by the depth of her yearning for him. Embracing his pillow, she allowed herself to relive the too-brief rapture they'd shared. Her fingertips tingled as though his mouth caressed each of them. In memory, she was once more swept by the intensity of their passion.

"Oh damn you, Sam!" she cried aloud, flinging the pillow away from her. It shouldn't have happened. Yet she knew very well she would do it all again without ever questioning her reasons.

It was after noon when Carol finally arrived to share her coffee. She seemed almost dazed with happiness, and Meg had no need to ask where she'd spent the night.

"I'm making progress," was all she said, but she never stopped smiling. To Meg's relief, she was so absorbed in herself she never thought to question Meg about her sudden disappearance from the party.

Carol sat down at the table where sunlight spilled across the gold-checked tablecloth. Dreamy-eyed, she gazed into the distance.

"I hope you come down to earth in time for the

performance tomorrow," Meg said with a knowing smile.

Flushing, Carol flashed her gamine grin at Meg and quickly changed the subject. "Dr. Worth has arranged a trip to the Grand Canyon next Sunday. Want to go?"

"Maybe." *Not if Sam's going,* she thought.

"Sure you do," Carol insisted. "He's taking a college van so there's plenty of room for anyone who wants to go along. We'll leave at the crack of dawn, though, since it's a three-hour drive."

"I'll see." Meg hoped Carol would be satisfied with the vague reply.

But Carol eyed her in a speculative way. "Why not go? How many chances will you have to see the Grand Canyon? They say the north rim is even more spectacular than the south where all the peasants go."

"Trying to appeal to my snobbery?" Meg asked with a laugh. She saw from Carol's intent scrutiny that she had no intention of dropping the subject. "I'm not going to spend an entire Sunday sight-seeing with Sam," she told her flatly. It was going to be difficult enough to face him tomorrow at rehearsal, as well as all the weeks of performing ahead. "He may be my director, but at least I can avoid him on my day off."

"'The lady doth protest too much, methinks,'" Carol quoted, giving her a sly look. Reaching across the table, she took Meg's hand and looked searchingly into her eyes. "The marriage may be over, but you're still in love with the guy, aren't you?"

It all spilled out then, all the pain and anguish Meg

had sworn never to share with anyone. Carol's warm and caring presence had broken the floodgates. Meg alternately wept and laughed as she told of the New York years, the hated modeling, the building resentments and the final bitter blowup that ended the marriage.

When she had finished, she wiped her eyes and said, "Sorry. I didn't mean to lay all that on you."

"What are friends for?" Carol asked, her voice husky with sympathy. "I've leaned pretty heavily on you about Payton this summer, haven't I?"

"And now that's going to be all right, isn't it?" Meg asked, relieved at the change of subject.

"Who knows?" Carol shrugged, and her eyes were shadowed. "One night of lovemaking does not a future make." Her attempt at a laugh was shaky. She stood up and reached for the coffeepot.

Standing, Meg reached out to hug Carol. For a long moment they stood there together finding there was comfort in friendship when love seemed elusive.

ALEX HAD BEEN ANNOYED when Meg told him she was going to the Grand Canyon with Dr. Worth and his wife. "I thought we'd spend Sunday together, and have a swim and dinner at my place."

In the predawn coolness of Sunday morning, Meg's mouth tightened at the memory of his words. Frowning, she slipped a tan poplin jacket over her bright blue knit shirt. Alex didn't own her, or her time. His increasingly possessive attitude unsettled her. He might be the perfect escort, or suitor, or whatever he was, but she was still free to make her own decisions.

By a series of subtle inquiries made through Carol, Meg had finally determined who was to go along on this trip. Zach claimed he intended to sleep all day. Joan had been to the canyon many times, so she declined. Carol reported that Sam planned to spend the day working on his play. So there would be the Worths, Payton and Carol, Walter McGrath and Meg.

The van was in the apartment-house parking lot, lights on, motor running. Through the dim morning light, Meg could see Payton helping Carol into the vehicle. Hurrying across the lot, she stepped into the van. With a shock that seemed to knock all the breath from her lungs, she found she had to climb over Sam's long legs to get to her seat.

"We're off," Dr. Worth announced as Meg settled herself between Sam and Walter.

They were in the middle seat, Payton and Carol in back, and the Worths in front. Meg stared at the back of Mrs. Worth's tinted hair styled in a 1950s bouffant, and wished herself far away, anywhere but sitting here with Sam's shoulder pressing against hers.

"I didn't think you were going on this trip," Meg said in a low accusing voice.

"You know me—" he gave her a careless grin "—I never pass up an adventure."

As Dr. Worth drove up the canyon road, Meg kept her eyes straight ahead, almost unaware of the banter going on around her. There were other routes to the Grand Canyon. Why did Dr. Worth have to choose the one passing Navaho Lake? He stopped at a viewpoint above the lake for Walter to take pictures. Everyone got out and Meg was forced to join them.

Below the cliff, the sapphire waters of the lake sparkled in the rising sun. Along the farther shore Meg could just make out the lighter green mass of the aspen grove, the flower-starred grass beneath the trees buried in shadows. She was achingly aware of Sam standing beside her, looking out over the lake. He was dressed in faded jeans, with a red shirt-collar showing above his ubiquitous gray sweat shirt.

"Beautiful, isn't it?" he asked, almost as though he had never seen it before.

Meg couldn't answer. She could feel his eyes on her, yet couldn't bear to look at him. Turning away abruptly, she led the others back to the van.

The mountain drive wound through groves of aspen and stands of pine, broken now and then by flowered green meadows. Eventually, they descended into a long valley lined with ranches. Then they were down in desert country, with sandstone bluffs in violent unearthly shades of coral and ocher and ivory.

The highway ascended from the desert floor to the Kaibab Plateau and a deep forest of tall ponderosa pines. At one point they passed a wide meadow where white-tailed mule deer grazed peacefully.

Passing the park entrance, Dr. Worth announced, "We'll stop at Cape Royal first because it's my favorite view of the canyon."

The roadside as they drove was a tangle of

growth. pine, scrub oak and wild locust trees drip-
ping with pink blossoms. The sweet fragrance of the
locust floated through the open windows of the van.

At Cape Royal, the group walked toward the
viewpoint, Walter adjusting his camera, Dr. Worth
explaining the geology of the canyon to Sam.

The view was so unexpected, Meg gasped aloud.
The rocky path through the pine trees, then suddenly
the world dropped away at her feet. Infinity appeared before her, light and shadow flowing among
the towering buttes, layer on layer of them in endless
procession. Lavender and red, brown and coral,
cream and gray layered in myriad variation...the
very skeleton of the earth exposed. A hush fell over
the group as they stood in silent awe of the immense
wonder spread before their eyes.

Her heart pounding with emotion, Meg grasped
the railing. She felt, rather than saw, Sam standing
beside her. Then his hand lay on the railing beside
hers. Face taut, she stared straight ahead, fighting the
urge to cover his hand with hers.

Once they would have shared this soul-stirring
spectacle by the touch of hands, a depth of glance.
Shared moments came back to her: a fiery, all-
enveloping sunset at Cape Cod, which they had
watched until last light died in the dark ocean, a
hushed Connecticut woods on a winter day, and a
tree filled with migrating cardinals like flames against
the new-fallen snow. Today they stood side by side,
lost in a scene of infinite distance, time and depth,
each one of them painfully alone.

Sam drew a deep ragged breath. Involuntarily Meg

turned to meet his eyes, seeing her own awe and wonder reflected there.

"There aren't any words," he whispered.

"No." Her throat was filled with emotion.

When they turned to walk back to the van, she let him take her hand in his. He was the best companion she'd ever known, she thought, enjoying the feel of his warm hand holding hers. With a lift of her spirits, she decided to let the past and future go and just enjoy this day.

On the way to the lodge, Dr. Worth regaled them with hilarious stories about the incredible mishaps that had taken place in past festivals.

Sam had the greatest laugh she'd ever heard, and Meg turned to smile at him. It was deep and warm, seeming to come from the very depths of his feelings. Drawing in a deep breath, she realized she couldn't be near him like this without being drawn to him. The same intangible magic that had ensnared her the first time they were together remained unchanged, undamaged by all the hurt they'd caused each other.

"Well..." Dr. Worth said, wiping tears of mirth from his eyes after enjoying one of his own stories. "I often wonder where all our performers go after the season ends. Some we never hear of again, others go on to make real names for themselves in the theater." Meg almost laughed aloud, he was so very much the little professor. "What are the future plans of this group?"

"Back to the university," Payton replied with a grin. "I plan to start producing some Shakespeare if I can talk the trustees out of their money."

"Good for you." Dr. Worth laughed. "Carol?"

"I'm halfway through a master's degree," she smiled, with a sideways glance at Payton. "Can't quit now."

"Back to Villanova," Walter grinned. "Unless some producer is so impressed by my talent he insists on mounting a Broadway production just for me."

There was silence until Dr. Worth prompted, "Meg?"

She shrugged. "I did a TV pilot early this spring. Maybe it will be picked up and I'll become a household word." Her laugh sounded hollow to her own ears, as she wondered whether she really wanted the TV series.

"I didn't know that." Sam gave her a quizzical look. "What's it about?"

"Top secret." She laughed. "Actually the plot is so preposterous you wouldn't believe it if I told you." She paused, acutely aware of Sam's body so close to hers, the scent of his shaving lotion, the dear freckles on his large hands. "What are your plans, Sam?" In spite of her effort, her voice was shaky.

He was silent for a moment as though considering. "My agent sent me a couple of scripts to read. Whether they'll go or not is the usual Broadway story." He looked at Meg, his eyes darkening, and she quickly looked away. "Then there's the possibility of the Guthrie. . . ." His voice trailed off.

As though sensing the need for a change of subject, Payton quickly turned the conversation to a discussion of regional theater.

The huge stone lodge at Bright Angel Point was

perched at the edge of the canyon, surrounded by tall ponderosa pines. The immense lobby was finished in hand-hewn logs, its floors and walls graced by colorful Navaho blankets. Floor-to-ceiling windows looked out on the incomparable view.

Dr. Worth led them out to the sunny stone terrace, which looked across to the South Rim. Far below they could see Phantom Ranch beside the pale gleaming ribbon that was the Colorado River.

"Perhaps we should go our separate ways from here," he said. "Let's all be back at the van by three o'clock."

Everyone murmured agreement. Giving Meg a meaningful wave, Carol immediately disappeared down the trail with Payton. Walter was busy setting up a tripod for his camera. Dr. and Mrs. Worth strolled away into the lodge.

"You're stuck with me," Sam said grinning down at her.

"I'll try to bear up under the strain." Her voice was teasing, but a sense of unease broke through her relaxed mood.

"Now just follow me and watch your step," he said, putting on an air of self-importance.

Laughing, Meg nudged him with her elbow. "Is this what's known as the blind leading the blind?"

"Deflated by an expert," he complained with a chuckle. "Come on, maybe we can get lost together." Taking her hand in his, he led her down the rocky twisting Bright Angel Trail.

There were occasional vista points along the way, with rustic benches hewn from pine logs. They paused at each one. There was no need for words. The infinite breathtaking beauty of the canyon surpassed anything she'd experienced. And it was fun being with Sam like this again. They'd often hiked together at the seashore or at his parents' home in Connecticut.

The last vista point before the trail descended to Phantom Ranch stood far out into the canyon. Meg paused there, breathless. The sun moving westward cast deep shadows in the depths now. Once more, the scene burst upon her with such power that she stood stock-still, enthralled.

A moment later, Sam stood beside her, their shoulders touching. For what seemed an eternity they stood there on the edge of the precipice, then turned to look into each other's eyes. Meg saw her own wonder mirrored in his face. *Oh, God,* she thought. . .*if only*. . .*if only.*

Slowly they came together, Sam's arms enfolding her, his mouth seeking hers. "Sam," she murmured. Their kiss was as powerful as the beauty surrounding them, and they remained locked in each other's arms until a troop of Boy Scouts came tramping down the trail. "It's a long climb back to the lodge," Meg said breathlessly. "We'd better get started."

"MEG, we're home."

With a start, Meg sat up. She'd fallen asleep on the ride back from the Grand Canyon, her head pillowed on Sam's shoulder. His voice was warm and close to her ear, his smile fondly amused by her sudden awakening.

Descending from the van, the sleepy group

thanked Dr. Worth and his wife. Stretching and groaning, they made their way into the patio of the apartment complex. It was nearly eleven since they'd stopped for dinner at a small country café, but there were still people sitting around the patio.

At once, Joan came bouncing toward them. She wore one of her peasant-style dresses, its skirt swirling around her voluptuous figure. In her hand she held a sheaf of papers.

Weary-eyed, Meg stared as Joan threw her arms around Sam.

"It's great, Sam. Absolutely the most powerful scene you've written yet." Joan took his arm, smiling greetings at the rest of the group. "But listen, there are a few things you need to fix. It'll be easy if we get to work on it right away."

"Tonight?" Sam protested, giving Meg a pleading sideways glance. "Joan. . .I'm bushed."

"Right now!" Joan insisted. "Otherwise I'll lose the thrust of what I want to tell you." Pulling on his arm, she led him away. "I have some stuff in my apartment I've written down that I think you might want to add to the scene. I'm sure you'll agree. . . ." Her voice faded as Sam allowed himself to be led toward Joan's apartment.

He gave one last backward glance toward Meg, who tightened her lips angrily and turned away.

Damn Joan! she thought as she unlocked her apartment. *The interfering bitch!* It had been a glorious day. She and Sam had been so close, shared such fun, just like old times. At dinner in the little café, catching his warm glances, she'd known he'd want to make love to her when they were back at Forest Grove. With all her being she'd wanted that, too, longing to share with him an ultimate climax to their emotion-filled day together.

Why was she damning Joan? Sam hadn't resisted Joan's assertive demands. If Meg had been important to him this night, he would have told Joan to get lost. He'd have come here to share a glass of wine and make love. Perhaps it would have been one step toward mending their relationship.

THE NIGHT's performance was a good one, with an enthusiastic audience and a gratifying number of curtain calls for the cast. Afterward, Sam walked down the tunnel toward the dressing rooms, complimenting his crew as he went. The huge room was a madhouse, with performers at the tables under the lights removing makeup, shouting for help with costumes, discussing the performance at the top of their voices.

At once his eyes sought Meg. She'd brushed him off with bitter words this morning. He didn't blame her. Yielding to Joan's demands that they work on the damned play immediately had been as frustrating as stopping in the middle of lovemaking. That's what the whole day at the Grand Canyon had been—a prelude to lovemaking.

Damn! Joan was a good sort. Her criticism of his third act was valid and helpful, but she shouldn't have let her enthusiasm carry her so strongly.

The moment when he'd caught up with Meg at the vista point still haunted Sam. The depth of her eyes darkened by emotion, the utter aloneness of her slender figure standing there on the edge of eternity, clung to his mind. *Oh God,* he thought . . . *if only* . . . . *Fool,* he berated himself. If he couldn't mend the relationship somehow, he must find a way to stop wanting her, stop hoping, stop loving . . . and sign the damned divorce papers.

He crossed the room to her. She had already removed her makeup and changed into a raspberry-colored skirt and a pale pink silk blouse. When she looked up at him, her eyes were suddenly shuttered, their hazel-green light dimmed.

"Hi, Sam." The voice was carefully noncommittal.

"Good performance, Meg. You get better all the time, love."

"Don't call me 'love,' " she replied coldly.

Sam felt something in him recoil as though struck by an icy wind. "Sorry." Regaining his composure, he used a voice as cool as hers.

"I have to go." Meg flung a pink sweater around her shoulders. "Alex!" she called and waved to the man who stood across the room looking for her.

Seething, Sam turned hostile eyes on Meg. "Alexander the Great again?" There was a sick feeling in the pit of his stomach. The thought of Meg in another man's arms seemed to tear his insides into bleeding shreds. *"Droit de seigneur,"* he said caustically. "The Lord of the Manor summons the village maiden to his bed."

Meg gave him a scathing look, then quickly made her way through the crowd toward the smiling Alex.

A sick feeling pounded at Sam's temples. Couldn't he say anything right? Every time they were together he came off sounding like a mean-spirited jealous bastard. *And that's just what you are,* he told himself furiously, as he pushed his way out of the dressing room, wanting only to be alone with his pain.

12

THE LEAVES of the huge maple tree shading the theater courtyard rustled softly in the warm August breeze. Meg sat on the shady deck behind the theater where the actors relaxed between scenes at night. Across the sweep of green lawn, on a grassy knoll beneath the pine trees, Alex was teaching his seminar to a crowd of fifty or more.

He has such presence, Meg thought, he could have been an actor. She admired the way he moved, the faint rise and fall of his deep resonant voice. Despite his increasing pressure for deeper involvement, their relationship had continued unchanged during the past month. Why was she so reluctant? Meg asked herself. Seeing him there across the lawn, so handsome and self-possessed, she knew he could have his choice of women. No doubt he had, in the years since his divorce. Whether because of the divorce or other reasons, she realized that Alex was not interested in long-term commitments. Maybe that's why she held back, unwilling to settle for a few months or a year living a Sybaritic existence as his mistress.

With a sigh, Meg leaned back against the rough lumber wall of the theater, stretching out legs clad in bright plaid madras slacks, her white linen blouse cool in the warm sun. When she chose to be honest with herself, she knew well enough why her feeling for Alex had never developed beyond pleasant companionship. The reason's name was Sam Richardson. No matter how she tried, she couldn't free herself of him emotionally. Too many nights she awakened to lie sleepless, sick with longing for him.

In the weeks since they'd shared that happy day at the Grand Canyon, Sam had maintained a carefully professional facade. Well, she told herself with a shrug, he'd obviously accepted the fact that they were through. She closed her eyes tightly as a familiar pain washed over her. Memory of the intense moments they'd shared at the canyon replayed in her mind. He'd thrown all that away because Joan had asked him to.

"Hi, Meg." It was Carol, looking jaunty in a green polo shirt and khaki shorts, a terry sweatband holding back her bright hair. "Waiting for Alex?"

Glad for the interruption of her gloomy thoughts, Meg smiled as Carol sat down beside her. Lately she hadn't seen as much of Carol as she had during the first part of the season. Payton, of course.

"Yes," she answered. "He wanted me to help him plan the cast barbecue at his place this weekend."

"Shakespeare's birthday party?" Carol laughed.

Meg grinned, amused by Alex's little conceit about the party. "He knows it's not really Will's birthday, although it's sort of the festival's birthday. Anyway, it's a tradition. He does this every year."

Carol didn't answer for a moment. She was staring across at Alex. "He is a great-looking guy, Meg." She glanced at Meg, then quickly away. "But not as great as Sam."

"Cool it, Carol." Meg's voice was brusque.

"Sorry." They smiled at each other in understanding. Then Carol's grin widened. "By the way," she said in an overly casual tone. "I have a bit of news. Payton and I decided last night to get married."

"Carol!" Meg cried out and flung her arms around her friend. "That's wonderful. When? Where? Tell me!"

"We're going to wait until we're home in Washington. I'd like my family with us." She hugged Meg enthusiastically. "Oh, I could just explode with happiness."

Even as she returned Carol's hug, delighted with this joyful realization of all Carol's hopes and dreams, Meg felt a flash of envy. Did this kind of happiness come only once in a lifetime?

Quickly she covered her pain at the thought of never again knowing the kind of love she'd once shared with Sam.

"You can take the credit, Meg." Carol brushed happy tears from her eyes and sobered. "It all happened because of the advice you gave me."

"What advice?" Meg stared at her in surprise. She didn't usually offer friends advice on their love lives. Her own failure in that department was too obvious.

"That I should tell Payton the truth about my feelings. When I finally got up the courage to do it, he confessed he'd held back because of the difference in our ages. Couldn't believe I'd want to marry him. And he's so straight arrow he wouldn't ask me to settle for anything less." She sighed happily. "Oh Meg, he's so wonderful."

"And so are you." Meg reached to hug her again.

Returning the hug, Carol said seriously. "You should take your own advice, Meg."

"What do you mean?"

"Have you ever told Sam the truth about your feelings, Dear Abby?"

"Of course I have. That's why we're no longer married."

"There are none so blind as those who will not see." Carol's tone was exasperated. "Have you *really* told him how you resented making your career second fiddle to his? Or how much you hate modeling? Did you ever mention the auditions you missed in order to earn money to live on? Meg . . . if Sam knew how you felt, well . . . ."

"It's too late." Meg's voice was as cold as her heart felt. "Too late to make it right again, Carol. You can't go back, you know."

DURING THE BRUSH-UP REHEARSAL for *Othello* the next morning, Sam blew up at her. It was the first time since the Grand Canyon that they'd exchanged more than the necessary civilities.

"Good Lord, Meg!" He was almost shouting as he stood up and walked to the stage apron. "Just because you gave a good performance last week doesn't mean you can sleepwalk through this one. Put some fire into it."

Furious at being called down before the whole cast, Meg turned to stare down at him. The cold look he gave her pierced her heart more than anything he might have said.

"Let me try it again," she said and stepped back offstage, fighting tears. Sam was right, of course. She was walking through the part today. She hadn't slept last night. Her mind kept veering wildly from Carol's words of advice to Alex's pressing insistence that she decide about going to Greece with him, to the ultimate and bitter knowledge that she'd lost the one man she really loved.

When the rehearsal ended, Meg exited backstage, hoping to avoid meeting Sam. A pleased-looking Zach caught up with her. "That was uncalled for," he said, eagerly sympathetic. "You should have put that arrogant ass in his place."

"His place is director," Meg snapped, tired of Zach's continual troublemaking. Looking him in the eye, she added, "We seem to have an abundance of arrogant asses here."

With an expressive shrug, Zach turned to speak to someone else. Joan touched Meg's arm.

"Don't let it bother you, Meg. Sam's been pretty uptight with everyone lately."

Except with you, Meg thought, hating herself for the jealousy roiling inside her.

"The season's nearly over," Joan continued pleasantly. "Like all of you who aren't returning to the safe confines of a university, Sam's concerned about the future."

"Tell me about it," Meg replied, and walked away. She was at once ashamed of her behavior. Joan had never been anything but friendly toward her, and she'd promised herself she'd behave the same way in return. But Joan's words indicated Sam had shared his feelings with her. That hurt so much Meg couldn't bring herself to make a conciliatory gesture toward the woman who'd taken her place with Sam.

And how many other women had there been in the past year? Surely a man like Sam wouldn't live a celibate life. The thought was so devastating she heard herself gasp. Even now, even when she was sure it was all over between them, she couldn't bear to think of him lying in another woman's arms.

THE ENTIRE CAST AND CREW had been invited to Alex's traditional barbecue. They made a colorful sight, Meg thought, watching them mill around the terrace and the swimming-pool deck. Nearly everyone was clad in western-style clothes—jeans, boots, cowboy shirts. Some of the women wore ruffled peasant-style skirts. Meg and Carol had indulged themselves with a shopping trip to the local western-clothing store, coming home with new brass-studded jeans, bright plaid western shirts and cowboy boots.

Meg stood by herself in the shadow of the terrace, sipping a glass of white wine. A three-piece combo alternately played western tunes and golden oldies. A few couples were dancing on the terrace.

Looking around at the crowd, Meg didn't see Sam. She was annoyed with herself when she realized he was the one person she wanted to see.

Carol and Payton were talking with some of the festival board people who had also been invited. Meg recognized Nedra, the blond woman who had been

Alex's date that first night she met him. She looked lovely in her white cotton-and-lace Mexican dress and heavy turquoise-and-silver jewelry.

Carol glanced up, her bright eyes catching Meg's. She waved. After a moment she began making her way through the crowd toward Meg.

Grasping Meg's arm, Carol grinned. "This guy knows how to throw a party. The wine is flowing like, well, like wine."

"Oh, yes," Meg replied, determined to summon up a real party mood. Where was Sam? And why did she care? She was Alex's guest, picked up and delivered in his Mercedes and treated like royalty. Sam hadn't even asked if she was going to be here. Giving Carol a dry smile, she said, "It helps to hire everything you need done for you."

Nodding in an absent manner, Carol turned to gaze at the group she'd just left. "Do you know that blonde, Nedra? She's 'old family' around here, so she told me."

"I've met her." Meg gave Carol a puzzled look. "I guess she had something going with Alex at one time."

"Boy, did she!" Carol said in low vehement tones. "I get the impression she's determined to have him." She sighed and gave Meg a dubious look. "You know me, Meg, honest to a fault."

"Honest, brave, loyal, steadfast—all those good Girl Scout things," Meg replied with a laugh.

"I swear I'm not being catty or anything. But I am your friend, so just keep quiet while I pass on some gossip for whatever it's worth."

"Don't bother," Meg said, feeling a sudden coldness rush over her. "Zach has been plying me with the details of Sam and Joan's romance."

"Zach is an ass," Carol answered with a dismissing wave of her hand. "No, it's Nedra. Someone mentioned your name in our conversation and she made it clear she thinks you're 'Alex's little actress for the season.'"

Meg drew in a sharp breath, glancing at Alex across the pool, moving among his guests, looking elegant in a tightly fitted plaid western shirt and tan slacks. "Tell it all," she said, her voice shaking.

Carol clasped her hand comfortingly. "That Nedra is a bitch, but I did gather that Alex likes to play the field. I decided you should be forewarned." She leaned closer to Meg. "I wouldn't hurt you for anything. I hope you're not really in love with Alex. I kept thinking you might do something foolish just because of what's happened to you and Sam."

For a long moment, Meg stood feeling as isolated as though she was on a mountaintop. The noise and chatter of the party swirled around her, unheard.

"Meg." Carol's voice seemed to come from a distance. "You aren't in love with him, are you?"

"No." She felt very cold and detached. She knew with absolute certainty that she did not love Alex Martin—never had and never would.

A burst of laughter caught her attention. There, across the terrace, stood Sam, his head thrown back, his rugged face alight with amusement; his lean body comfortably attired in western jeans and red-checked shirt. *My love*, she thought, looking at him. *My one and only love.* As though the words sped across the space between them, he looked up, caught her eye and gave a casual wave. *My once and only love,* she corrected herself.

"Meg, are you okay?" Carol looked concerned.

Struggling for control, she managed a laugh. "Thanks, friend." With a chagrined look, she added, "Would you believe Alex almost had me convinced to barter my body for a trip to the Greek islands?"

"Not you, Meg," Carol replied with conviction.

"You're right. I'd have finally said no." Meg squeezed Carol's hand and gave a fake sigh of resignation. "You'll have to admit it would be tempting."

"Sure," Carol agreed, then added, "And I may be tempted to tear out all that bleached-blond hair if Nedra doesn't quit coming on to Payton."

"Hi, you two." Sam sauntered up to them, his hands in his back pockets. Meg didn't dare look at him. Just standing this close to him was intensely disturbing. With an effort she maintained her poise, sipped her wine and let her eyes roam over the crowd.

"How's my favorite hunk?" Carol asked with a laugh.

"Don't toy with me, woman," Sam grinned. "Payton has already warned me that he has an exclusive." He reached out to draw Carol close to his side.

"Persistence pays off," Carol said happily.

"Congratulations. When's the big day?"

"Well...." Carol's face was alight with happiness. "At first we thought we'd look for the nearest justice of the peace. But I have this superstition, silly as it sounds, that if we start off with a lot of fanfare it will last forever."

"Maybe so," Sam agreed, glancing at Meg. "We started with a justice of the peace."

Torn by a flood of memories, Meg's hand tightened around her glass. That remembered joy totally possessed her for a moment. They had barely had enough money to buy the license and pay the justice of the peace. When the final words were said, they'd stood for a long aching moment, only their hands touching, drowning in each other's eyes. Sam had whispered as he finally bent to kiss her, "My love. For all our lives."

"Oh!" Carol looked stricken and clapped her hand over her mouth. Meg was jolted back into the present.

"I'm sorry," Carol moaned. "I didn't think. When will I learn to keep my mouth shut?"

"No harm done," Sam said genially, giving her another hug.

"Of course not." Meg gave them a wry smile. "Our relationship must have caused a lot of awkward moments this summer." *It's nearly over,* she thought, trying to quell the hurting inside her. *I may never see him again, never know again the joy we once shared. And we thought it would be for all our lives....*

"That's some understatement." There was an undertone of meaning in Sam's voice. Meg refused to acknowledge it, or to look at him.

Flushing, Carol glanced away and spotted Payton gesturing for her to join him. "Look at that," she laughed. "I think he needs rescuing from Nedra." Quickly, she walked toward him.

An awkward silence fell. Meg stared into her wineglass. Sam jammed his hands in his back pockets and rocked on his boot heels. Finally he cleared his throat, surveying the milling throng of people. "Pretty classy affair. Nothing but the best booze...combo...tons of food, steaks no less." When Meg made no reply, he continued, "You seem to fit right in, love. You'd make a great hostess for His Honor."

Irritated by his baiting, Meg shrugged and lifted her chin defiantly. "It shouldn't be too difficult to grow accustomed to this kind of life."

Sam's easy grin faded, the blue eyes darkened with anger. "I'll bet," he said harshly. "I'm sure the life-style of Alexander the Great must be very seductive. It doesn't bear comparison with the way you lived with me."

His mask of geniality had vanished. With all her strength, Meg struggled to maintain control, wanting him, hating him for hurting her. Her whole being seemed torn apart.

Turning to confront her, Sam's voice dropped, bitter and low. "Why are you wasting your time with that playboy? He's a dabbler with no real commitments. What makes you think you could be happy with someone who simply smooths out the difficulties in his life with money?"

Taking a deep breath, he went on. "A great poet once said that the lust for comfort murders the integrity of the soul. I think that describes your friend, Alex."

"Stay out of my life," Meg said in as cold a voice as she could muster. Miserably, she refused to meet his eyes. His words were made even more hurtful by the knowledge that he was absolutely right in his evaluation of Alex.

"Hi!" With his usual flair for arriving at the wrong moment, Zach interrupted them. "You look right at home in western clothes, Sam." His dark eyes glittered with malice. "You could play a cowhand without a single change."

Meg managed a tight smile. She was sick of Zach forever gossiping about Sam, and now coming out with an obvious put-down. Her voice was hostile. "I'm sure Sam could be anything he wanted to be," she said in a bright, too-loud voice.

"Anything but your husband." Sam's voice was low, close to her ear.

Looking quickly at Zach, Meg saw that he hadn't overheard Sam. He was busy scanning the crowd. Dizzy with the pain of her emotions, Meg thought resentfully that she had defended Sam only to have him turn his derisive comments against her.

"Where's your paramour tonight, Sam?" Zach asked with a leer.

A flash of anger lit Sam's eyes. He covered it with a short bark of laughter. "There are so many, Zach. You'd have to give her a name before I could answer that question."

"Ah, here she comes now." Zach ignored Sam's words. "The luscious Joan, ready to start drooling over you, as usual."

"Knock it off, Zach." Sam's tone was more than a little irritated. With an impatient gesture, he walked away to intercept Joan and lead her toward the bar.

"See what I told you?" Zach sounded triumphant.

Meg scarcely heard him as she watched Sam take a cocktail from the bartender and, smiling, hand it to Joan. A surge of jealousy almost blinded her. Knowing Zach was watching her, she kept her expression bland and uninterested. She'd never disliked him more than she did at this moment, standing there, actually gloating. She was relieved when Walter McGrath joined them.

Only half listening to their conversation, Meg let her eyes follow Sam and Joan until they disappeared in the crowd. Alex was coming toward her, and Meg drew a deep breath. She would be polite to him through the interminable hours of the party that lay ahead. Then it would be over, as she had always known it would be.

It didn't matter that this would be the end of their relationship. Her feeling for him had never had any real depth. He could never be a part of her heart, her soul, her very being as Sam had been.

"They're serving the steaks," Alex said, taking her hand possessively in his. With Zach and Walter, they strolled toward the line formed at the barbecue.

As they joined the line, Nedra turned to give Meg an appraising look. Her cheeks grew hot as she wondered how many people Nedra had convinced that she was "Alex's little actress." If only she could simply disappear. The fact that Nedra's gossip was untrue made it all the more infuriating. Meg wondered whether Alex knew . . . or even worse, Sam. Ignoring Nedra, she decided she would not be disagreeable. She would simply walk through the rest of the party as though she was playing a part onstage. Carol's motives had been above reproach, but Meg knew it would have been easier to remain ignorant of the gossip about her.

Their plates loaded with steak, barbecued beans and salad, Meg and Alex found a place at one of the long tables decorated with red-checked tablecloths and candles in hurricane chimneys. To Meg's dismay their table companions were Nedra and the mousy older man who was her escort; the Worths, Carol and Payton, and two couples who were on the festival board. Glancing around, Meg wondered where Sam was, for Joan was at a table with Zach and Walter.

Feeling completely detached from the conversation, Meg stared at her plate, knowing she could not choke down a bite. Alex filled her glass with burgundy from the bottle sitting on the table. Without looking at him, she picked it up and took a sip. She could feel his thigh pressed against hers where he sat on the bench next to her. Quickly, she moved away.

"It's been a remarkably successful season," Nedra was saying in a cool silvery voice.

"Indeed!" Dr. Worth agreed heartily.

"With a good deal of credit to my favorite actress here." Alex smiled fondly at Meg and covered her hand with his in a possessive manner.

At once Meg caught the significant glances exchanged along the table. Even the placid Mrs. Worth was looking at her in a meaningful way. *Good Lord*, Meg thought. *They all believe I'm sleeping with him, that we're having an affair. Does Sam think so too?*

"When are you leaving for Mykonos, Alex?" someone asked.

With a proprietary air, Alex put his arm around Meg's shoulder. "I'm afraid that all depends on Meg." There was such overweening confidence in his tone, Meg could not restrain herself from giving him a sharp look.

"Really, Alex dear," Nedra drawled. "Isn't that carrying your summer entertainment a bit too far?"

Alex looked annoyed. A flush spread over his face.

An embarrassed silence fell at the table. Meg's hands were trembling with repressed fury. When she set down her wineglass, the liquid slopped onto the tablecloth.

Shrugging off Alex's arm, she stood up and glared at Nedra. "I've had quite enough of your bitchy insinuations, Nedra," she said in a low furious voice. "Just to set the record straight—" and her glance swept around the table "—despite the rumors Nedra's been spreading, I have not been sleeping with Alex." To her horror she realized her voice was rising, that she was totally out of control. "We're friends, nothing more."

Everyone at the table was staring at her in shock.

Then she caught the look of pained humiliation on Alex's face. He didn't care that Nedra's gossip had hurt and shamed her. She was causing a scene...she was making waves on the smooth sea of his life. With a look that told her they were no longer friends or even acquaintances, he turned away, his face set in cold lines. Sam was right...the man had no integrity.

Oh God! she thought suddenly. *I have to get out of here, quickly.*

Curious heads turned to stare after her as she ran across the terrace and through the house. Stumbling in the unaccustomed cowboy boots, Meg started up the lane, determined to walk back to the college.

"Meg!" Someone was following, and she walked faster. Then Carol and Payton were there, each taking one of her arms, bundling her, sobbing, into Payton's car.

13

"IT'S A GORGEOUS MORNING," Carol said when Meg opened the door. She stood there holding a coffeepot and two mugs, smiling broadly. "Let's have coffee on the patio."

Looking beyond her, Meg saw with relief that the patio was deserted. "I feel like going into hibernation," she told Carol with a pained grimace. "I made such a fool of myself last night."

"I thought you played a great scene," Carol laughed. "I'll bet Nedra was never told off like that before."

Meg groaned, feeling her face turn scarlet with embarrassment.

"Forget it," Carol urged sympathetically. She waved a hand toward the table, empty and inviting in the cool shade. Morning sunlight laid intricate patterns on the flagstones as a slight breeze stirred the leaves of the oak trees.

"Payton's meeting with Dr. Worth this morning," Carol added. "He's thinking of doing summer Shakespeare at the university, so he wants to learn everything about it. Come on...." She turned toward the table.

Quickly slipping into white shorts and a sleeveless

red T-shirt, Meg pinned her hair up in a loose twist. She almost hated to meet her own eyes in the mirror. Never in her life had she done anything as totally disgraceful as her verbal attack on Nedra last night. Yet, when she met those reflected eyes, a slow satisfied smile spread across her face. Chagrined she might be, but she felt vindicated. A vicious gossip like Nedra should be confronted, but she wished it hadn't taken place in public. Sam had accused her of being temperamental and explosive. He must be convinced of it now.

By the time she joined Carol she was again feeling a bit embarrassed. With a sigh, she dropped into the chair opposite her friend.

"You'll feel better after you have your caffeine fix," Carol said with a grin. Then she sobered. "You okay this morning?"

"Sure." Meg said it airily. "I told you I didn't plan to slit my wrists."

She didn't add that the brandy Payton had offered after they brought her home had practically knocked her out. In spite of that, she had awakened early, with plenty of time to agonize over the scene she'd caused. She was embarrassed by her behavior, but just as furious with Nedra and Alex. He'd certainly shown his true colors. She was well rid of that relationship. Fervently, she hoped she never had to see him again.

"Good morning!" said a cheery voice. Joan sat down at the table, carrying her own steaming cup of coffee. Her blond hair was drawn back in a ponytail and she wore a cool-looking flowered shift. "I can't believe there's only one week left in the season," she said. "The summer has flown so fast."

Not for me, Meg thought. To her, the summer had been one long emotional struggle, with time creeping painfully by.

All too obviously avoiding any mention of the party last night, Joan began inquiring about Carol's wedding plans. Meg leaned back, sipping her coffee, enjoying Carol's infectious enthusiasm.

As that subject dwindled, Joan accepted a refill from Carol's coffeepot. "I feel absolutely slothful," she said with a laugh. "No rehearsal this morning. I can't decide what to do with myself."

"No rehearsal?" Meg glanced at her watch. "I can't believe Sam, the perfectionist, would cancel even a brush-up rehearsal."

"He's not here."

Carol and Meg stared at Joan in surprise.

"You don't mean he's gone permanently... for the season?" Carol was carefully not looking at Meg.

"Oh, no!" Joan raised her eyebrows. "I thought everyone knew. Sam flew to Minneapolis last night. They're going to make a final decision on the new Guthrie director. He really wants the job, you know." She gave Meg a long searching look.

Meg turned away. There'd been hurt enough for a lifetime in this season, but this last hurt seemed the most devastating of all. Sam had wanted this directorship badly, and now he'd gone to the final interview without even mentioning it to her. Joan knew. She bit her lip so hard it hurt. Sam had shared his hopes and dreams with Joan, not with her. *And why not,* she reminded herself miserably. *I rejected him in every possible way.* Even the few happy times they'd shared this summer couldn't erase that truth.

"That's why he left the party early?" Carol asked, with a covert glance at Meg.

"He drove to Las Vegas last night to catch the plane." Smiling, Joan raised her crossed fingers. "Let's hope he gets the job."

Then he missed my big scene, Meg thought. Looking at Joan's blandly smiling face, Meg was certain he'd be enlightened about her public display of bad manners as soon as he returned.

"Isn't that your phone?" Carol interrupted.

Jumping up, Meg hurried to answer it. For one unreasoning instant there leaped inside her the wild hope that it might be Sam calling from Minneapolis.

"Open the champagne, honey!" Jerry Greene's familiar voice burst in her ear when she lifted the receiver. "Your pilot has been picked up."

"Jerry—that's great news." At once she realized how flat she sounded.

"Hey there! A little more enthusiasm. I've got the contract right here on my desk. How soon can you get back? They plan to start taping right away. Pilots aren't usually bought this late in the year."

"The festival has another week to run, Jerry," Meg replied, wondering why she wasn't more excited by his news. "I can't possibly leave now."

"Oh, come on!" Jerry objected. "You wouldn't want to lose this part for some two-bit summer-stock contract. There must be an actress there who'd love to take over your part."

You didn't talk that way when I wanted out, Meg thought resentfully, wishing she could lash out at him for having condemned her to this long agonizing summer.

"I always finish what I start, Jerry," she said, taking a deep breath. She was suddenly determined she would not leave the festival until the end. In that instant she knew it was not just finishing out the season. Everything between her and Sam had to be finished too, one way or another.

"Hey, Meg!"

"No," she interrupted decisively. "I'm going to complete the season here, Jerry. If you can hold the part for me, I'll do it, and you know I'll do a good job."

"But hon, that's not the point. They're in a rush to shoot some episodes in time for the fall season."

"If they won't wait for me, you'd better start looking for something else for me to do." Then she added, "But no modeling, especially not for George Harmon."

Unexpectedly, Jerry laughed. "Honey, the commercial is great. I saw it last week. But I'm not sure George wants to work with you again. You disappointed him so much he even asked about your sexual preferences."

"He just couldn't believe I'd turn him down." She giggled, remembering George's shock when she refused his advances.

Jerry chuckled. "George couldn't recognize class if it hit him in the head. Don't worry about it."

"I don't intend to, but I do intend to finish the season here."

"Final word?" Jerry asked in a pleading tone.

"Final," Meg said firmly. "Do what you can and let me know."

"Okay, hon, but take it from me, you can't plan on a series waiting for you."

"Who cares?" Meg said lightly. When she hung up, she stood dumbfounded by her own reaction. It would have been the easy way out, to fly off to L.A. at once, never having to face Alex or Sam again. She knew she couldn't leave the festival in the lurch now, although Dr. Worth might be glad to see her go after her behavior last night. She simply liked to finish what she started. Everything except marriage. The idea came flashing through her mind, leaving a deep aching pain behind.

Suddenly she realized she hadn't once considered the money the series would bring. It had been the farthest thing from her mind. With an ironic smile, she wondered what Sam Richardson would think about that.

SAM TOYED with his coffee cup, staring out the windows at the heat waves rising from the runways of Chicago's O'Hare airport. Beneath the sense of satisfaction and the gratifying knowledge that he'd be director of the renowned Guthrie Theater next year, there ran an undercurrent of restlessness. All the success in the world couldn't be enough without Meg to share it.

Glancing up, he watched Meg's father threading

his way through the tables of the coffee shop. Pleased to see him, Sam realized Meg had inherited a lot of her looks from Ben Driscoll. Even at sixty he maintained a trim youthful figure. His graying beard was short and neatly trimmed, his head quite bald. The dark hazel eyes were enough like Meg's to bring an ache to Sam's throat.

Rising from the table, he held out a hand in greeting. Ben gripped the hand with both of his, looking at him intently.

"Good to see you, Sam. So glad you called." The voice was deep and sincere.

Sam grinned, clapping the older man on the shoulder. "Thanks for coming in to help me through this two-hour layover. Sorry Ginny couldn't make it." He was genuinely glad to see his ex-father-in-law. Although they hadn't seen each other since the Driscolls' winter holiday in New York, they kept in touch by telephone. Right now, Sam felt a deep sense of gratitude that their friendship had survived, despite the end of his marriage.

Ben sat down and smiled at the waitress who appeared to fill his coffee cup. "You know Ginny, always off doing her own thing. She's directing this new play, *Spirit*. As she flew out the door, she was bemoaning the fact that she'd like to discuss something with you about directing."

"Tell her to call me," Sam said, taking the menu from the waitress. They quickly agreed that even an airport coffee shop couldn't ruin a grilled-cheese sandwich and each ordered one.

Sam imparted his news about the Guthrie appointment and accepted Ben's effusive congratulations. Then he listened with interest to Ben's amusing adventures teaching Shakespeare in inner-city Chicago this summer.

"What else have to you been up to?" Ben asked as the waitress returned with their sandwiches.

Startled, Sam gave him a questioning frown. Was it possible Meg hadn't told her parents they were working together this summer? "Doing a little Shakespeare myself," he replied slowly. "I've been directing *Othello* at the Forest Grove Shakespearean Festival."

"Forest Grove!"

She hadn't told him. The shocked expression on Ben's face was proof enough.

Ben set his sandwich down. "With Meg?"

When Sam nodded, Ben's eyes lit up and he grinned hopefully. "You and Meg." Then his grin faded into a puzzled frown. "I wonder why she never mentioned you were there."

"I can guess," Sam replied dryly. Both Meg's parents had become his dear friends. The divorce had shaken them badly, just as it had his own family who adored Meg, but blindly blamed her for hurting Sam. After he first heard the news, Ben had called him, sounding completely devastated. Since then, every time they'd talked there had been subtle and not-so-subtle hints about reconciliation. If Ben had known they were working together, no doubt he'd have pressed harder. Meg knew that. She was simply avoiding the problem.

Shaking his head morosely, Ben stared out the window. "You and Meg," he muttered. His eyes met

Sam's in a piercing look. "You were meant to be together."

Sam tried to dismiss the pain those words aroused. "I know it and you know it. Unfortunately, Meg doesn't agree."

"What happened, Sam? Really happened?"

He wasn't prying, Sam knew. Ben simply cared deeply about his daughter—and his friend, Sam Richardson.

As he'd learned to appreciate the qualities of Ben Driscoll, Sam had often thought there were few men so caring. Not many would give their summers to teaching underprivileged kids the joys of Shakespeare. When Ben received the Teacher of the Year Award, Sam and Meg had flown in from New York to attend the ceremony. The emotional evidence of all the lives Ben had touched left Meg and Sam both in tears.

Strangely enough, he and Ben had always discussed the divorce in a roundabout manner. Now Ben was demanding explanations.

Sam gave him a cynical smile. "I guess I'd like to say it's all her fault."

"It takes two," Ben replied succinctly.

"Yeah." Sam grimaced, looking down at his untouched sandwich. "It takes two." Despairingly, he added, "I've never signed the divorce papers. Not that it's brought her back to me. . . ."

Trying to choose his words carefully, trying to control his emotions, Sam told him about Linda, about the money he'd borrowed for the play, about the final explosion, and his aborted attempts to persuade Meg to start over.

"That wasn't the only reason she left," Ben told him flatly.

Sam spread his hands in a despairing gesture. "That's what she told me. What else could it be?"

Sipping his coffee, Ben looked thoughtful. "How important was Meg's career to you?"

Staring at him in surprise, Sam frowned, then said defensively, "I cared about her career. She wasn't Cheryl Tiegs, but she was a top model, and she is a damn good actress."

"She hates modeling." Ben shook his head wonderingly. "And you didn't know that?"

There was a sinking sensation in the pit of Sam's stomach. It had been so easy to blame Meg for their breakup. Now Ben was quietly offering him a share of the blame, and it wasn't going to be easy to take.

"You know . . ." Ben leaned back in his chair, studying Sam's face. "A lot of people think I'm a patsy because I've made it easy for Ginny to do her own thing. She never wanted the big time, like Meg. In fact," he added ruefully, "she wasn't good enough. But she loves the work she does, and that makes me happy, too. Understand?"

Shaking his head, Sam wondered what Ben was trying to tell him. "Meg isn't like her mother . . ." he began.

"No," Ben agreed. "She's always had her goals set high, and she's responsible and organized."

"And unreasonable," Sam added, aware of the bitterness shading his voice.

"She wanted to be an actress." Ben's voice was firm. "She never, ever wanted to be a model. She did that for the money."

"Oh, hell!" Sam buried his face in his hands. She'd never mentioned her aversion to modeling, never complained, until the end when she'd thrown the whole blame in his face.

"She never told me," he muttered, and knew at once he was merely justifying himself. Thinking back, he realized he hadn't wanted to know she was unhappy with her work. She'd sent plenty of signals, and he'd ignored them, insisting to himself that their life was exactly what they both wanted. He remembered how she was always so exhilarated after a theater performance. But after a long day of modeling, she always seemed drained.

"That was her big mistake," Ben said with a shrewd look. "Just think about it for a minute, Sam. Whose career always came first? Who never had to pass up an opportunity in order to pay the rent?"

The words were like the proverbial salt rubbed into a wound. Sam slumped in defeat. "In other words, you think I'm a selfish son of a bitch—and I am."

"Hey, son. . . ." The compassion in Ben's face only intensified the ache in Sam's chest. "You're the only guy I want to see married to my daughter. The two of you need to stop thinking only about yourselves. Think about each other." He grinned. "It takes two."

"Right," Sam agreed through the pain clutching his throat. "But only one of us wants to mend it." His fists clenched angrily. "She's got another guy—a rich one—after her now. Every time we're together she flares up at me."

"That's good."

"What?" Surprised at the words, Sam made a choking sound.

"If she didn't still care, she wouldn't still be angry." Ben smiled. "And if she wasn't still in love with you, she'd have told me you were at Forest Grove. It wouldn't have mattered enough to keep it secret."

Silent, Sam stared at the encouraging smile on Ben's face. His hopes had been dashed so many times this summer. Even with the insights Ben had forced on him, how could he make Meg see that they needed each other, that they were meant to spend their lives together? How could he make her love him again? Maybe it was too late already. Alex Martin's lifestyle had to be pretty damned tempting.

"I'm rooting for you," Ben told him as they shook hands at the airline gate later. Ducking his bald head, he gave Sam a twinkling look. "How about if I tell Ginny we're spending Christmas in Minneapolis?"

"Hold that thought," Sam grinned, suddenly buoyed with hope.

14

THE AUGUST BREEZE carried the sound of voices as Meg walked toward the grassy knoll where Alex held his seminars. Her nerves tightened. She had hoped to avoid him. But it was not Alex leading the seminar, it was the overburdened Dr. Worth.

"Oh boy!" she breathed softly, wondering where Alex might be. Had she blown everything apart when she lost control and made a scene at the party? Surely it wasn't important enough to make Alex withdraw his support from the festival. She'd even apologize to Nedra rather than let that happen.

Remembering the look of distaste on Alex's face after she'd exploded at Nedra, Meg was certain she'd never see him again. She'd done the unforgivable: she'd made Alex uncomfortable. Watching Dr. Worth obviously enjoying himself with his audience, Meg knew it didn't matter. Her relationship with Alex had been pleasant, but it would leave no ripples in her life.

"How come Dr. Worth's teaching the seminar?" she asked Carol as she dropped down on the bench beside her. Carol was sitting on the deck behind the theater, reading a book and munching on an apple.

With a quick glance toward the seminar group, she

gave Meg a mischievous smile. "His majesty, Alexander the Great, has flown off to the Greek isles, so I understand." She chuckled. "One guess why he decided to leave town so quickly."

"Oh, no!" Meg groaned. "I hope I didn't get Dr. Worth and the festival in trouble."

"No sweat," Carol replied easily, taking a bite of her apple. "Payton just happened to be in Dr. Worth's office when Alex called. He thinks Alex enjoys being the big man at the festival too much to ever withdraw his support. Not even after being embarrassed by one actress making a scene. Dr. Worth is being supremely diplomatic, I might add."

"You might also add that I'll never be invited back." Meg gave her a rueful look.

"Well, you're off to bigger and better things, anyway," Carol replied.

"Sure," Meg answered doubtfully. She told Carol she was certain she'd lost the part in the TV series because she'd refused to leave the festival before it ended.

"Damn!" Carol exclaimed. "When things go wrong, they really go, don't they?"

"Never mind," Meg told her. "Something will come up." Without thinking, she let out a long sigh. "Is Sam back yet?" Meg caught the sympathy in Carol's eyes and looked away.

"I hear he'll be back for the last *Othello* on Saturday." Tossing her apple core into a waste container, Carol stood up. "Almost time for rehearsal." She paused, looking directly at Meg. "It's been a momentous summer, Meg. Not the least of it was meeting you."

Tears stinging her eyes, Meg reached out to hug Carol and be hugged in return, knowing she had made a friend for a lifetime. "It's not over yet." She wiped the moisture from her eyes. "We've got three days and three plays to go through."

WHEN HAD HE ARRIVED? Meg wondered as the cast gathered in the theater for the last rehearsal of *Othello*. Sam was sitting on the stage apron, long jean-clad legs dangling, his gray sweat shirt beginning to fray at the neckline. He seemed happy and self-confident. No doubt Joan knew what had happened in Minneapolis. If anything could have convinced Meg she and Sam were through, it was the fact that he had said nothing to her about the trip to Minnesota.

"Settle down, everybody," Sam called. He asked for a run-through of scenes where the timing had slipped at the last performance, or the emphasis had been lost. The work went smoothly, but everyone seemed subdued with the melancholy that always accompanies the closing of a show.

As they began to break up after Sam dismissed rehearsal, Joan took the center stage.

"Our modest director—" Joan said, with a mocking bow in Sam's direction "—is too shy to share his good news. So I want to make an announcement. . . ." With a flourish of her hands, she announced in ringing tones, "May I present Mr. Samuel Richardson, new director of the famous Guthrie Theater in Minneapolis."

There was a burst of applause. At once members of

the cast crowded around Sam, congratulating him, asking questions. He stood among them with easy confidence, grinning, shaking hands, running his fingers through his rumpled hair.

Watching, Meg's heart plunged in despair. Sam had shared nothing of this important event in his life with her. He'd shared it with Joan, who seemed to know everything about him. *It's over, lady,* she told herself bitterly. *Better stop brooding and get on with your life.*

It was only polite to add her congratulations, so Meg waited. He kept glancing at her over the heads of the people surrounding him. It seemed to her there was a certain self-satisfaction in his face, as though he couldn't wait to say to her, "I told you so." She wondered if Joan had already confided to him that Meg had put on an incredible display of temper at Alex's party.

Oh God, she thought suddenly. *I can't bear to talk to him or even be near him.*

Whirling around, she dashed out of the theater. For an instant she thought she heard Sam's voice calling her name, but it was drowned in the chatter of the cast who were still discussing Sam's appointment.

DURING THE AFTERNOON, her doorbell rang insistently. Huddled in bed, Meg pulled the pillow over her ears and refused to answer. All she wanted was to be alone. It was the only way she could hold herself together until tonight. She should have obeyed Jerry's summons to L.A. Right now, she'd probably be at work in the studio.

Sam had been gone when she made that decision. She suspected now that it wasn't her vaunted sense of responsibility that caused her to make it, but her desire to see Sam again. Well, she'd seen him and she'd managed to keep her feelings under control until Joan happily made her announcement. At this moment, Meg thought that if Sam came near her, touched her, or even spoke to her, she would surely shatter into a million pieces.

She finally knew just how terribly she loved him, knew that she had never really stopped loving him. There was no point denying it now that it was ended. Maybe she'd never love another man, but somehow she had to put her life back together without Sam.

Loneliness engulfed her as the afternoon light intensified beyond the bedroom window. Soon she'd have to get up, go to the theater and perform. Sam would be there, too, backstage, at the rear of the theater or in the dressing rooms. She wondered whether she could maintain her composure long enough to get through the night. It was the last performance of *Othello*. She wanted it to be the performance of a lifetime. With a sob, she realized it would be her farewell gift to Sam.

"Meg!" Carol's voice interrupted her gloomy thoughts, along with a prolonged pounding on the door. Throwing on her robe, Meg went to answer.

With a questioning frown, Carol asked, "Are you all right? Sam's been worried about you. Where have you been?"

"Right here," Meg answered. Then a lie stumbled from her lips. "It must be some kind of virus...

headache, shakes." She had been trembling uncontrollably when she climbed into bed, but it was from emotion, not infection.

"What can I do?" Carol's voice was solicitous.

"I'll be okay." Meg felt relieved, knowing she'd just found a way to avoid Sam. "I wanted to rest so I could perform tonight."

Next, Sam arrived. Meg wouldn't have answered the door, but she thought it was Carol returning.

"I hear you're under the weather," he said, his deep blue gaze searching her face. Meg nodded, hoping she appeared sufficiently pale and wan.

"Anything I can do?" He pushed the door open a little farther.

"No," she said quickly, holding the door firm. "If I stay in bed, I can make it through the performance."

"I really wanted to talk to you, Meg," he began.

She interrupted. "Sam, I feel awful. Some other time, please?"

"Sure." Reluctantly, he began to back away. "Can I bring you anything, do anything for you?"

"No. I'll just rest."

He nodded, looking so concerned she wanted to weep. When he didn't move, she finally had to close the door on his worried face.

"Damn!" she muttered as she climbed back into bed and picked up the novel she had been trying to read.

If only, if only. . . . Those two words seemed to keep recurring in her thoughts. If only Sam wasn't so caring as he had been just now. If only she could blame him for all their problems. There it was! The thought she had never allowed to come into her mind—the thought that perhaps Sam wasn't entirely to blame for their parting.

Throwing the novel across the room, Meg lay back against the pillow, folding her arms over her aching eyes. All during their marriage, she realized, she had played the role of martyr, passing up offers for plays that might have furthered her career, but didn't pay much. Harold had once taken her to task for turning down a script, but she couldn't tell him the real reason any more than she could tell Sam. Why had she never confided to Sam how much her work in the theater meant to her, or how deeply she hated modeling? Instead, she'd suffered in silence and destroyed their relationship in the process.

Oh, she'd been noble, wanting him to be free to succeed. But she'd been wrong in giving up the same right for herself. Sam had never asked her to do that. He must have been totally unaware of the anger building inside her. It was the stupid kind of self-sacrifice she always hated to see in other women.

Or men, for that matter, she thought, remembering how she'd often felt her father sacrificed for her mother's little theater commitments. She'd blamed her mother for her absences and her devotion to the theater group. She suddenly realized that her parents had an extraordinary marriage, one with both freedom and commitment, each doing the work they loved, with a center of love and appreciation to hold it all together. The fact that she and Sam had never arrived at that enviable arrangement was not his fault alone.

Restlessly she got up from the bed, pacing through the small apartment. Insight seemed to pile on insight. Worst of all, she knew with certainty that Sam had never been unfaithful while they were married. She'd acted like a jealous shrew, blaming him because Linda was coming on to him. Even if she hadn't walked in on them, she was sure now that Sam wouldn't have succumbed.

As for the loan from Sam's father, it had been a business arrangement between the two of them and none of her concern.

She'd rushed blindly off to Los Angeles, then rushed into the divorce without ever really trying to work things out. Now it was too late.

Choking back a sob, Meg returned to the rumpled bed. What good did it do to hide here? She assured herself it was a matter of surviving until she could leave Forest Grove.

There on the dresser was her purse with the airline ticket to L.A. sticking out of it. Suddenly she knew she wasn't going back to live in Los Angeles. She'd stop off long enough to clean out her apartment. Then she was going to New York, back to legitimate theater. The fulfillment she'd found in her work this summer proved she belonged onstage, not in front of a camera. If the money was less, it didn't matter anymore. She'd be doing the work she loved, with her satisfaction in that, not money.

The decision seemed to lift a great weight from her shoulders. So much so that when a worried Carol arrived bearing a large bowl of steaming chicken soup, Meg burst into laughter.

IT WAS GOING to be a triumph, Meg knew. For the last time, she quickly changed into the body stocking and the nightgown Sam had insisted on. The audience was spellbound, their gasps and groans at moments of high drama indicating how deeply they were caught up in the world of *Othello*. A kind of electricity seemed to leap from the stage as the actors moved through the play in perfect rapport.

Meg paused before the mirror at the end of the tunnel, checked her makeup under the lights there, then hurried up the stairs to the stage. Only the dim backstage lights were on. Taking a deep shaky breath, Meg waited in the wings.

"Meg?"

Sam! She felt his warmth close beside her and she trembled with a sudden sweep of emotion. In the melee of preparation there hadn't been a moment when he could have approached her until now. His big hand closed over hers, and love for him filled her with longing and with pain.

"You're superb," he said softly, close to her ear. "You are going to be a great actress, love. Nothing can stop you now."

Her throat clogged painfully as he lifted her hand to his lips, kissing the fingertips in the old loving way. A bottomless yearning suffused her whole being.

"Onstage, Meg." It was the stage director, hurrying through the half dark.

Without a word, Meg moved away, reluctantly releasing Sam's hand. Like a sleepwalker, she made her way to the stage and arranged herself on the bed.

Desdemona would die now, and Meg felt something inside her die, too. Sam's words had sounded like a farewell. "Nothing can stop you now."

Slowly the stage lights came up. Torches flickered at each side of the stage apron. Expectant silence from the audience permeated the scene.

Zach entered, wearing the Moor's brilliant seventeenth-century robes, speaking his soliloquy as he vows to kill the beloved wife who he's certain has betrayed him. He moves across the stage and bends to kiss Desdemona, then cries out in pain:

"'One more, one more...be thus when thou art dead, and I will kill and love thee after. One more and that's the last: So sweet was ne'er so fatal. I must weep, but they are cruel tears. This sorrow's heavenly; It strikes where it doth love.'"

"'Who's there? Othello?'"

Desdemona awakens, welcoming her well-loved husband. Grown mad with jealousy, Othello tells her she must die. She pleads with him, trying to convince him of her innocence.

"'It is too late'" he cried.

The audience gasped as Othello held the pillow over the face of his struggling wife. At last she was still.

A painful constriction bound Sam's chest. Othello's last words echoed in his brain. "It is too late!" Beloved Meg...beloved wife...it is too late. He wanted to turn away from the awful scene that seemed to have such parallels in his own life, but the intensity of emotion projected from that stage held him immobile.

" 'My wife! My wife! What wife? I have no wife!' "
Othello cried out in anguish.

Sam's hands tightend into fists beside his tense
body. He was shaken to his depths by the sorrow of
Othello's loss . . . and his own.

Onstage, Othello descended into an agony of remorse and guilt. " 'Then must you speak of one that
loved not wisely, but too well . . . of one whose hand
like the base Judean threw a pearl away richer than
all his tribe.' "

Threw a pearl away. Tonight, Sam thought,
Shakespeare seemed to have written words meant to
sear Sam Richardson's soul. I loved her, but I didn't
understand her. . .and I threw away the only pearl of
my life.

As the last speeches echoed through the theater,
Sam drew a deep ragged breath. With a rough gesture, he wiped the tears from his eyes and moved
backstage.

15

THE STAGE LIGHTS went dark. There was a brief silence, then applause burst from the audience like a thunderclap. At once they were on their feet, shouting, "Bravo! Bravo!" The stage lights came up and the entire company moved through the carefully choreographed bows, curtsies, smiles.... Again and again they were called back by the enthusiastic spectators.

Running gracefully to the stage apron to take Zach's hand for another bow, Meg felt a wild sense of exhilaration. The moment was headier than a bottle of champagne, more satisfying than anything short of lovemaking. It was the theater, her true love. She knew she had given her finest performance, achieving a height of excellence she'd wanted for Sam as much as for herself.

At last the applause died away and the houselights came on. It was over.

Backstage, Zach turned to her, holding both her hands and looking at her almost affectionately. "You're the greatest, Meg. There isn't any part you can't play."

Surprised by his emotional outburst, Meg looked at him, dumbfounded. Then he added, with his usual arrogance. "I wanted you to be the first to know that I've been offered a part in a terrific new play on Broadway . . . uptown."

"Oh Zach, that's wonderful!" From the corner of her eye she saw Sam watching them over the heads of the people surrounding him. "I'd kiss you, Zach," she said, forcing a light tone. "But I'm fighting a flu bug. Mustn't spread it around."

"Later?" he asked with a laugh, wiggling his eyebrows suggestively.

"Later." She gave him a smile. Quickly threading her way through the throng to the dressing room, she narrowly avoided Sam.

Sitting at her dressing table, Meg began to remove her stage makeup. The room was filling up now, the noise level rising as the exhilarated players savored their triumph. It was over, she thought, creaming her face, and she wasn't sure whether she was sad or relieved. The intense feeling she'd experienced in the last scene returned, only briefly suppressed in the joyous response to the audience reaction. It was truly over. As Carol had said, it had been a momentous summer, with all their lives changed irrevocably.

In the mirror, she caught the image of Sam watching her from across the room. He looked preoccupied, as though he didn't even hear the people talking to him.

Farewell, Sam, she thought sadly, then straightened her shoulders. What the hell! She was not going to skulk back to her apartment just to avoid a confrontation with Sam. She'd go and enjoy the cast party and kiss Sam goodbye along with everyone else. If her acting wasn't good enough to carry that off, she'd better turn in her Equity card.

Yet, as the costumes were hung up for the last time and the crowd begin to thin out, she guessed Sam was waiting for her. He hadn't moved, standing there against the farther wall, accepting the kisses of his female cast, handshakes and congratulations from the crew.

Meg frowned. She still didn't want to be alone with him. With a sense of relief, she saw Dr. Worth approach Sam, then lead him away, talking and gesticulating.

Hurrying now, Meg brushed out her hair, letting it fall in a soft dark cloud around her shoulders. She finished removing her makeup, then slipped into a paisley-printed full skirt in autumn colors with a matching long-sleeved blouse. Gathering all Desdemona's accessories into the basket provided for them, she placed it beside the costumes hanging on the pipe rack. Gently, she let the soft material of the diaphanous nightdress slide through her fingers... remembering.

The farewell party was already underway when Meg arrived in the courtyard. Tables were set up loaded with food, including a huge sheet cake bearing the legend: Congratulations on a Super Season. People were milling around exchanging embraces, kisses, forwarding addresses and toasts to the future.

"Feeling better, Meg?" Carol squeezed her arm.

"Oh, yes." Meg smiled.

"Enough for a glass of wine?" Payton asked, and when she nodded, went to get it for her.

The three of them laughed when Dr. Worth switched on the stage microphone. "He does love to give a speech," Payton grinned.

"How can I begin to thank you?" Dr. Worth said sincerely, looking around the crowd. "This is, and I mean it with all my heart, the greatest company we've assembled in all our twenty years. You've done Will Shakespeare and this festival proud. I salute you!" He lifted his wineglass in a toast.

He then insisted Carol and Payton come to the stage, where they were congratulated and toasted on their coming wedding. Payton took the microphone to thank the cast and crew of *Measure for Measure* for their cooperation and their fine work.

"Sam, do you have anything to say?" Dr. Worth gestured toward Sam who was standing across the courtyard from Meg.

With an eloquent shrug, Sam vaulted onto the stage.

Meg clenched her fists, fighting the ache that filled her chest. *How can I bear to never have you in my life again?* she asked silently.

"I will modestly say," Sam began, with that engaging grin of his, "that this may have been the most superb *Othello* ever produced."

Everyone laughed, applauded and cheered. "However," he continued, making a show of appearing modest, "little credit is due the director. I can only begin to express my gratitude to an incredible cast and the world's best crew. I've observed your growth as actors with pleasure." He took a deep breath, and his expression grew serious. "There are no words to describe the performance tonight. It was one of the most sublime moments in all my years in the theater."

He paused for a moment as though undecided, then continued. "Without taking anything from the rest of you, I'd especially like to praise my naive and tortured Othello...." He indicated Zach, who looked both surprised and pleased as the audience joined Sam's applause for him. "And of course, my evil Iago...." This time Walter grinned and bowed to the applause.

Sam's deep blue gaze met Meg's then, over the heads of the throng. Her whole being yearned toward him, yet she shrank from what he might say.

"I also had in my cast," and he hesitated for one long throbbing moment, his eyes devouring Meg's, "I had," and he paused again, "the most beautiful, most desirable, most loving Desdemona who ever gave her life to the jealousy of the misguided Moor. Meg...." He held out a hand toward her.

Nodding and smiling, Meg struggled to hold on to her composure. Tears pricked at the backs of her eyes, and her hand trembled so that she quickly set the glass of wine down on a nearby table.

"My thanks to all of you," Sam finished, and jumped down from the stage with easy grace.

Dr. Worth announced that supper was served, and people began to cluster around the tables. For a moment, Meg stood alone. Carol and Payton were the center of a group congratulating them, teasing, asking about their plans.

Unwillingly her eyes went again to Sam's lean

figure where he stood beside the stage, drinking a glass of wine someone had brought him. His tribute to her had seemed too emotional to be merely off-hand. Meg insisted to herself that she must have read too much into the words, feelings she longed to hear.

Joan, looking curvaceous and enticing in a clinging white dress, stood talking to Sam, her back to Meg. Sam was listening, a slight frown creasing his forehead. Then he looked across the courtyard at Meg. Suddenly he grinned, seized Joan by the shoulders and kissed her enthusiastically.

It was more than she could bear. Meg turned and fled.

Halfway across the dark tree-shrouded campus, she heard running footsteps behind her. *Oh, Sam!* She quickened her pace. *Just let me go. Let's not hurt each other anymore.*

Sam stopped beside her, slowing his pace to hers, almost strolling, his hands in his back pockets. Feigning a casual manner, he said, "Joan just told me you'd turned down a TV contract in order to finish the season here."

"So?" She managed to choke out the word.

"Why?"

There was a brief silence while Meg regained control. "Because what I've done this summer has been more satisfying to me than anything I've done in my career." She turned to face him. "I'm going back to New York to start over. Now I really know what I want to do with my life." Deep inside, her heart cried, *I want you, Sam...more than anything on earth.*

"So you're going back to starving in a garret." His voice was so low she couldn't be sure whether he was being sarcastic.

Meg shrugged. "If that's what it takes."

"What about Alex?" There was a pained tentative quality to the question.

"Don't tell me Joan hasn't informed you about my faux pas at the barbecue? Too bad you missed it."

"So Carol said," he replied with a sharp laugh. "Claimed it was one of your greatest scenes."

"Well...." She let the word trail off. What more was there to be said between them? she thought miserably. Only farewell.

"Meg." Suddenly Sam stood still, reaching out to take her shoulders in his big gentle hands. Moonlight shadowed his craggy face, hiding his eyes from her gaze.

Immobilized by his touch, she waited. She loved him so, and now her heart lay in shreds knowing he would never love her again.

"I saw Ben when I went through Chicago," he said in a too-casual tone.

"Oh?" she said carefully. "That's nice." *Why?* she wondered. *Why doesn't he just let me go out of his life, and my parents, too?* She sensed he was struggling for words, but she remained silent, holding her emotions in tight rein.

When he spoke, his voice sounded thick. "I've finally realized how much your acting career means to you, Meg. It was rotten and unfair of me to let you play second fiddle all that time. You were right on target when you called me selfish." He paused for a long moment, and when she didn't reply, he asked in a low tentative voice. "Is going back to New York what you want to do most?"

Meg hesitated. How could she say that what she wanted most was to be with him, especially when he'd just publicly displayed his affection for Joan. But her answer was honest. "No . . . it's just the best alternative."

In the moonlight she saw him frown at her as though he didn't understand her meaning. "Why did you leave the party just now?"

It was the one question she would have wished to avoid answering. But hadn't she decided that honesty was the only path to take from now on?

"I wasn't interested in watching you play a love scene with Joan." In spite of her efforts to control her voice, there was a bitter note in the words.

"That was no love scene, Meg. She just told me you weren't going back to L.A. It meant so much to me, I guess I got carried away."

"Sam. . . ." She tried to move away from him, but his hands held her firmly in place, their warmth on her shoulders arousing old longings.

"Joan's been helping me edit the play," he continued. "That's all. There's never been anything between us, any more than there was ever any relationship with Linda." His finger tilted her chin and he turned so that the moonlight flooded his anxious face. "Do you believe me, love?"

"Yes," she whispered hoarsely. "But Zach said. . . ."

Holding her away, Sam gave her a searching look.

A frown darkened his features. "Zach's been playing Iago to your Othello, hasn't he? Damn him! I guess that was his twisted way of getting even with me."

"Yes. I didn't know...." Her voice trailed off as she was seized by regret for all the pain her jealousy had caused both of them. She had wronged Sam just as Nedra had maligned her with false insinuations.

"I never signed the divorce papers, Meg." Sam's voice was low and intense, with a question in his tone.

"Sam, you idiot!" A laugh choked in her throat because she wanted to weep at the same time. "They'd have been final after a year anyway."

"The year isn't up." He looked deep into her eyes.

A tremor shook Meg as his meaning gradually dawned on her, and her heart leaped against her ribs.

It seemed an interminable time they stood, washed in moonlight, looking into each other's face. At last Sam began to speak, and Meg recognized Othello's words to his beloved Desdemona.

"'Perdition catch my soul, but I do love thee! And when I love thee not, chaos is come again.'"

"Sam!" The name burst from her throat with a sob. She was caught in his dear familiar arms, the lean body hard against hers, his mouth warm against her temple.

"Come to Minneapolis with me, Meg," he murmured. "Don't you know neither of us is whole without the other?"

"Yes...oh, darling! Yes!" A wild rush of joy filled her and her arms tightened around his broad shoulders. Tears spilled over, hot on her cheeks. "Sam, I love you so much, and I thought I'd lost you forever."

"My love...." His mouth claimed hers. All her being responded as the kiss deepened, seeming to weld their very souls together.

Slowly he released her, one hand tenderly smoothing back her hair. "They're going to produce my play at the Guthrie this winter," he said with his lopsided grin. "Without you it can't be done, because I wrote the lead for you."

"Oh, Sam," she said tremulously. "Were you so sure of me?"

"No." There was a catch in his voice and his arms clutched her fiercely against him. "Maybe I thought it was a way to lure you back to me."

"Dearest love," Meg murmured, laying the palm of her hand softly against his cheek. "You didn't need a lure. I just needed time to get my priorities straight."

Sam's arms tightened around her, his lips caressing her earlobe and the curve of her throat, sending tendrils of fire burning through her body. Lifting her face, she gave herself to him in a deep fulfilling kiss.

"I've been such a fool, Sam." She held his face in both her hands, looking at him with eyes of love. "I never listened to you and never told you how I really felt."

Smiling, Sam drew her close in his arms, his lean strength arousing the sweet warmth of desire. "Listen now, love...."

With his lips tracing fire along the edge of her cheek, he whispered, " 'Perdition catch my soul, but I do love thee.' "

THE AUTHOR

Elisabeth Macdonald moved from Utah to California after her marriage, where she fell in love with the Golden State's beaches and sunshine. Now that her two children are grown, she devotes most of her time to writing stories that offer "real insights into people."

Love Me Again was inspired by Elisabeth's visits to the Utah Shakespearean Festival.

INTRODUCING

Harlequin Temptation ™.

Sensuous…contemporary…compelling…reflecting today's love relationships! The passionate torment of a woman torn between two loves…the siren call of a career …the magnetic advances of an impetuous employer–nothing is left unexplored in this romantic new series from Harlequin. You'll thrill to a candid new frankness as men and women seek to form lasting relationships in the face of temptations that threaten true love. *Don't miss a single one!* You can start new *Harlequin Temptation* coming to *your* home each month for just $1.75 per book–a saving of 20¢ off the suggested retail price of $1.95. Begin with your FREE copy of *First Impressions*. Mail the reply card today!

First Impressions
by Maris Soule

He was involved with her best friend! Tracy Dexter couldn't deny her attraction to her new boss. Mark Prescott looked more like a jet set playboy than a high school principal–and he acted like one, too. It wasn't right for Tracy to go out with him, not when her friend Rose had already staked a claim. It wasn't right, even though Mark's eyes were so persuasive, his kiss so probing and intense. Even though his hands scorched her body with a teasing, raging fire…and when he gently lowered her to the floor she couldn't find the words to say no.

A word of warning to our regular readers: While Harlequin books are always in good taste, you'll find more sensuous writing in new *Harlequin Temptation* than in other Harlequin romance series.
® ™Trademarks of Harlequin Enterprises Ltd.

Exclusive Harlequin home subscriber benefits!

- SPECIAL LOW PRICES for home subscribers only
- CONVENIENCE of home delivery
- NO CHARGE for postage and handling
- FREE *Harlequin Romance Digest*®
- FREE BONUS books
- NEW TITLES 2 months ahead of retail
- MEMBER of the largest romance fiction book club in the world

Harlequin Photo Calendar

Turn Your Favorite Photo into a Calendar.

Uniquely yours, this 10 x 17½" calendar features your favorite photograph, with any name you wish in attractive lettering at the bottom. A delightfully personal and practical idea!

Send us your favorite color print, black-and-white print, negative, or slide, any size (we'll return it), along with **3** proofs of purchase (coupon below) from a June or July release of Harlequin Romance, Harlequin Presents, Harlequin Superromance, Harlequin American Romance or Harlequin Temptation, plus $5.75 (includes shipping and handling).

ANNE WEALE
SUMMER'S AWAKENING

Anne Weale, bestselling
author of FLORA and
ANTIGUA KISS, has written her most sensitive and romantic
novel ever — SUMMER'S AWAKENING.

A lifelong battle with her weight kept Summer Roberts insecure
and isolated, yet inside she was warm, passionate and desperate
for love. Computer tycoon James Gardiner's entry into her
sheltered world was devastating in more ways than one — through
his kindness and unintentional
cruelty she emerged a slender,
beautiful woman, sure of herself
and sure of her love....

Watch for **Summer's
Awakening** at your favorite
bookstore in August, or send
your name, address and zip
or postal code. along with a
check or money order for
$4.25 (includes 75¢ for
postage and handling)
payable to Harlequin
Reader Service, to:

Harlequin Reader Service

In the U.S.
P.O. Box 52040
Phoenix, AZ 85072-2040

In Canada
P.O. Box 2800,
Postal Station "A"
5170 Yonge Street
Willowdale, Ontario
M2N 5T5

FA-J